"Teacher would step on Anna," said Kirsty, becoming tearful again.

"Teacher would not," Andrea contradicted her, "Anna would already be trampled to death in the hall going to class."

Kirsty began sobbing aloud, with her mouth open. "Andrea!"

"Well, I think it's ridiculous. You know what she's like. Whenever she gets around people she pretends to be a chair or something. And she's good, too," Andrea said, with reluctant pride. "She even fools me, sometimes. I mean, what if somebody sat on her and squashed her flat? Imagine the embarrassment!"

"Andrea," Mother began threateningly.

"Mom, Anna is weird and you know it. There's a million things that could happen to her," Andrea said. "Look, why don't you teach her yourself?"

the woman in the wall

the woman in the wall

Patrice Kindl

Houghton Mifflin Company

Boston 1997

For information about this and other Houghton Mifflin
trade and reference books and multimedia products,
visit The Bookstore at Houghton Mifflin on the
World Wide Web at http://www.hmco.com/trade/.

The text of this book is set in 11.75 point Janson Text.

Library of Congress Cataloging-in-Publication Data

Kindl, Patrice.
The woman in the wall / by Patrice Kindl.
p.   cm.
Summary: Because she suffers from extreme shyness,
Anna retreats into herself and her secret rooms, where
she attempts to remain hidden from the outside world.
ISBN 0-395-83014-1
[1. Bashfulness — Fiction.   2. Self-confidence — Fiction.]
I. Title.   PZ7.K5665Wo   1997
[Fic] — dc20   96-24567   CIP   AC

Printed in the United States of America
BP   10   9   8   7   6   5   4   3   2   1

This book,
with the exception of Chapter 17,
is dedicated to my husband, Paul.
Rose and Joe get Chapter 17.
Thanks, you guys.

one

Hello.

My name is Anna. I am fourteen years old and a very shy person.

I don't know why I'm telling you all this. You probably have tons of better things to do than sit around listening to me.

What else do you want to know? I'm Anna and I'm shy. And fourteen. That's really all there is to tell.

Thank you.

Goodbye.

THE END

Oh! You're still there?

Oh, dear. Now I suppose I'll have to —

All right, I'm sorry. It wasn't really true, what I said. There *is* more to tell. If you're absolutely positive it won't bore you, I'll tell you the story of my life. So far, anyway.

I have always been shy. The urge to hide came over me at a very early age. My mother says I was a good baby; I never fussed at all. Both of my sisters came out of the womb with mouths wide open, screaming their heads off, their hands outstretched to grasp at whatever life offered. I, on the other hand, never even whimpered as I entered the world. I just lay there quietly in my incubator and tried to fit in. I had no longings for power or domination. I didn't want to intrude in any way; I simply wanted to blend into the scenery with as little fuss as possible. In this I succeeded.

"Where's the baby gone?" my mother would say, poking around in the crib blankets. "She's got to be right here; I put her there myself two seconds ago. Anna is a naughty girl, hiding from Mommy."

"Anna!" my mother's cry would echo from cellar to cupola. "Where are you, Anna?"

That was what she always wanted to know. Even today, all I have to do is close my eyes and say aloud, "Anna! Where are you, Anna?" and those long-ago days come to mind, perfectly clear in every detail. A tendency to disappear, you see, is and always has been my leading characteristic.

I don't really disappear, not exactly. I'm just not very noticeable. I'm small and thin, with a face like a glass of water. And I like to hide.

I believe that I inherited this trait from my father. I never really knew him. After a series of temporary vanishings, each longer than the last, Father faded out of our lives altogether, and we never saw him again. I was only three years old at the time.

I can't tell you much about my father, except that he bought a very large and dilapidated house for his bride, amassed an impressive collection of tools and materials with which to repair it, and then disappeared.

I don't think that it was the size of the job that frightened him off. No, I'm afraid that as the years went by he felt that the house, big as it was, was getting too full of daughters. He grew more nervous and jumpy, my mother says, after the birth of each child, and his absences became longer and more frequent.

My older sister, Andrea, remembers him best, and she says that whenever she entered a room where our father was sitting, he would duck behind a newspaper or book and sit perfectly still, apparently hoping not to be noticed. If she spoke to him, he would shut his eyes and hum quietly to himself.

"He had a retiring disposition," my mother said. "Like you, Anna."

We don't even have a good photograph to remember him by. Family snapshots show only an ear, or an elbow, or the back of his head, as he sidled crabwise away from the eye of the camera.

The last my mother heard of him was more than a year after he left. It seems that he had taken a job at the Library of Congress in Washington, D.C., and he'd given her name as a contact in case of emergency. They called her because my father was lost somewhere in the building and no one could find him. It's quite a large place, I understand, with something like two hundred and seventy miles of bookshelves. It's easy to see how a man like my father could get mislaid in a place like that.

The library guards swore he couldn't have left the building, but they never did find him. Eventually he was officially presumed dead by the authorities and our lives went on. I always liked to think that he was still alive in there, living off library paste and sandwich crusts from the staff's brown bag lunches. My mother says that that's just a fantasy and that we have to face facts, but it makes me happy to think of him like that, and after all, it *could* be true.

I did wish that he had stayed with us a little longer, that he had given me more of a chance to be a daughter to him. I believe that he and I would have had much in common.

I developed an interest in his tools when I was only a tiny girl. They were all I had of him, and I learned everything I could about their use and care. I know that most childhood experts do not recommend the unsupervised use of power tools by *very* young children, but I was remarkably mature for my age, and though small, very strong. I discovered that my hands were quick and clever, and that I enjoyed building and making things.

I also learned to sew. The lady who had lived in our house before us had been an accomplished seamstress and, before her retirement, had owned a small fabric store. When she died she left the attics filled with bolts of material, spools of many-colored threads, boxes of buttons and lace, and all sorts of craft supplies.

By the time I was seven years old our house was beginning to look like the grand old mansion it had once been, and my family was the best dressed in town. I have always been blessed, or cursed, with a seemingly endless fund of nervous energy. It is a real hardship to me to sit idle; I must be doing something. So I snipped and sewed and sawed and hammered to my heart's content.

I was proud to be such a help to my mother. She had a good job with an insurance company but, with a big old house and three young daughters, the money wouldn't have gone nearly as far without my efforts.

We were a happy family, or so I thought. I at least was entirely content to go on living exactly as we were, forever. But my mother had different ideas, it seemed.

"Anna, where are you?" my mother called to me one day. "Come out, darling. I need to talk to you."

Uneasily I crawled out from behind the sofa in the front parlor, where I had been peacefully engaged in attaching some fine old Victorian beadwork to the collar of one of Andrea's denim jackets. A nice effect, I thought. I didn't like it when Mother called me "darling." It usually meant bad news.

I presented myself, standing up straight so that she would be sure to see me. When she spotted me she patted the sofa cushion beside her. "Sit here beside me. So, darling," she said, avoiding my eye, "you're seven years old now, aren't you? Such a big girl!"

I regarded her with alarm. I was not a big girl at all, and we both knew it. I was an extremely small girl.

"Such a big girl," she repeated firmly. "You know, dear, school starts in a month. We'll have to start thinking about some new clothes for you as well as for Andrea and Kirsty."

I simply stared at her.

Andrea lunged into the room. She was ten years old and going into the fifth grade that year.

"What! You're going to send *her* to school? You can't."

"Stop bouncing at me like that, Andrea," Mother said. "Just sit down and be quiet for a moment."

"Anna, I want a pink dress with ruffles for the first day of school." Five-year-old Kirsty came in, trailing her doll Bethany behind her. "With those glittery things all over the top. Like Cinderella's ballgown."

"You are so stupid, Kirsty," Andrea said. "Nobody wears ballgowns to school."

"Andrea, please," said Mother.

"Just for the first *day*," Kirsty said, tears beginning to well up in her eyes.

"Kirsty, Andrea, I am speaking to your sister. Now, Anna," Mother said in a reasonable, kindly tone of voice that turned my knees to water, "you have to go to school. It's the law. You should have gone last year, or even the year before, but I didn't think you were ready. Girls!" she said suddenly, in a sharp voice. "You're sitting on your sister. I can't see her."

My sisters looked around themselves and shuffled their bottoms on the couch. I waved my arm to indicate that I was fine.

"Ah! There you are. You must realize, Anna, that this life you lead is not healthy. You haven't left this house in years. That isn't right for a growing child."

I shrank miserably into the couch. I couldn't possibly leave the house; it was like asking me to strip off my very skin.

"And you need to play with other children."

We were all silent after this pronouncement, trying to imagine me playing with other children.

"You could play hide-and-seek, for example," Mother said brightly.

Kirsty shook her head. "It's *boring* playing hide-and-seek with Anna. All you do is look and look and look and you never find her."

"I wouldn't be doing my duty as a mother if I didn't send you to school," my mother said, ignoring Kirsty. "I don't mean to frighten you, but the state could even come and take you away from me if I don't send you to school."

"Huh!" Andrea said. "If they came to get her, she'd hide. How would they ever find her?"

I decided that I had to say something.

"I think —"

"That isn't the point," Mother said to Andrea.

"I SAID, 'I THINK —'" I shouted in her ear. She jumped.

"Did you say something, Anna?" She leaned down to listen.

"I think if I have to go to school I will die."

She shook her head at the passion in my voice, but she looked away.

"She might, you know," said Andrea.

They all stared gloomily at a point on the sofa where they believed I was sitting.

"Teacher would step on Anna," said Kirsty, becoming tearful again.

"Teacher would not," Andrea contradicted her.

"Anna would already be trampled to death in the hall going to class."

Kirsty began sobbing aloud, with her mouth open. "Andrea!"

"Well, I think it's ridiculous. You know what she's like. Whenever she gets around people she pretends to be a chair or something. And she's good, too," Andrea said, with reluctant pride. "She even fools me, sometimes. I mean, what if somebody sat on her and squashed her flat? Imagine the embarrassment!"

"Andrea," Mother began threateningly.

"Mom, Anna is weird and you know it. There's a million things that could happen to her," Andrea said. "Look, why don't you teach her yourself?"

I brightened up. This seemed like an excellent idea.

She sighed. "Because I have to work, that's why, to keep food on the table."

"Well, okay, in the evenings," Andrea suggested. "I mean, come on, Mom. Anna's pretty smart. Bet she already knows more than any first-grade teacher. It'd be a cinch."

"I want Mommy to teach *me*," Kirsty said jealously.

"Yeah, me too, come to think of it," said Andrea. "That'd be great! No more school."

"Children! Now, don't be silly. It's true that Anna is an unusually intelligent child, but there's more than book learning to the first grade. What she needs most to learn is how to interact with other people. As for you two, it's out of the question. It's bad enough that I've been leaving Anna alone here while I work without leaving you as well. Anna at least is always perfectly behaved."

Andrea and Kirsty looked sulky.

"I wouldn't do anything," Andrea said.

"Me neither!" shrilled Kirsty.

"Oh ho, like fun you wouldn't do anything!" Andrea said. "How about smearing Mom's makeup all over the bathroom, huh? I guess you call that nothing?"

Kirsty took a deep breath and opened her mouth as wide as it would go. "AAAAAHH —"

"Stop!" Mother said, putting a hand over each of their mouths.

"Anna, I'm sorry," she said. "But what else can we do? You'll have to go to school like other children."

"*I* think you're being silly, Mom," said Andrea scornfully, prying Mother's fingers off her lips. "It's not like anybody would ever know."

This was a mistake. Mother's chin came up and her eyes flashed. She hated to be reminded of the fact that no one outside of our immediate family, not even the neighbors, believed in my existence.

"Anna," she said, "I admit that you are in many ways a very mature and clever seven-year-old, but you are still a child. I am your mother, and I say that you must learn to mix with other people for your own good." On a kinder note, she continued, "I will call the school today and tell them about you. Perhaps we can arrange something — special tutoring in a small class — something like that."

She stood up. "I must do what I think best," she said, and left the room.

"Gee, Anna," Kirsty said, clutching her doll to her, wide-eyed. "What are you gonna do?" but I didn't answer, because I had already crept back into hiding.

That night I started work on the secret room.

two

I didn't intend to defy my mother, not at first. I was an obedient child, anxious to win the approval of those I loved. I only wanted to hide from the *idea* of school. It hadn't occurred to me yet that I could hide from school itself.

The day after Mother informed me of her decision I heard her talking on the phone to someone named Mrs. Waltzhammer. Mrs. Waltzhammer, it seemed, was the school psychologist. She was to come to our house in two weeks to meet me and to Discuss The Situation.

"Now, Anna," Mother said when she got off the telephone, "it's very kind of Mrs. Waltzhammer to come to our house instead of seeing you in her office. So I'm expecting you to cooperate. I want you to speak up nice and loud so she can hear you. And maybe you should make yourself a new dress for the occasion. Something really bright and cheerful; something to give you a little color. What do you think?"

I fingered the mottled gray-brown material of my tunic and a tear ran down my cheek. I didn't want something bright and cheerful. I was proud of my clothing. I wore a loose overblouse that had been artfully cut and dyed to resemble a moth's wings, and underneath a pair of matching leggings. I have always admired the way moths can camouflage themselves against many backgrounds and have copied their coloration and outline in my dress as a tribute to their skill. I considered my outfit to be both graceful and practical.

"*I* think it'll be like watching the Invisible Man," said Andrea. "Mrs. Waltzhammer will just see this tiny little hot-pink dress floating around with nobody in it. No, I'm serious, Mom. I think a flashy outfit would make Anna fade out altogether."

"Well, Andrea," my mother said tartly, "what do you suggest, then?"

Andrea gave this some thought and then shrugged. "You could have a big flashing neon arrow that says 'ANNA' pointing at her chair, I guess. That's about the only thing that's going to do any good."

"Oh, Mommy, can we?" asked Kirsty, charmed with this idea. "I want one that says 'KIRSTY NEWLAND' over my chair. Anna, could you make one for me too?"

My mother threw up her hands in defeat. "Oh, wear what you like, Anna! I just thought that a brightly colored dress would help Mrs. Waltzhammer to . . . to locate you. Anna? I don't want you to hide from Mrs. Waltzhammer. I mean it, now."

What would happen if I did? I pictured this Mrs. Waltzhammer rampaging through the house like a vengeful tornado, flinging open closet doors, jabbing under beds with a broom handle, upending laundry hampers, relentlessly hunting me down.

I speeded up the schedule for construction of my secret room.

Ours is an old house, a Queen Anne Victorian built in the 1880s with the expectation of housing a large family and a staff of servants. It is known locally as the Bloodgood Mansion and has twenty-two rooms, not counting halls, bathrooms, enclosed porches, attics, walk-in closets, and cavernous linen cupboards.

I created the secret room out of plasterboard, two-by-four planks of lumber, and empty space. Our house had thousands of square feet of unused, unnoticed, unneeded empty space. The space I took for my secret room (really, it was a room and a passageway) was of no importance to anyone but me. So you really couldn't call it stealing, could you?

This was the most ambitious project I had ever attempted, but I had no doubt that I could carry it out. I am not a modest person. In fact, in some ways I'm afraid I'm horribly conceited. This may sound odd to you, coming from the mouth of such a shy person.

Well, it *is* odd; I don't claim to understand it. The very thought of a stranger's eyes upon me makes me faint with fear. My heart pounds in my ears, my hands shake, and I see spots in front of my eyes. Yet whenever someone looks right past me without seeing me, I feel myself infinitely superior to him. I laugh in my secret heart at his stupidity and hug my own quick-wittedness to myself.

Now, I know as well as you do that this is wrong. A really nice person would not think or feel this way. So I do my best to subdue my vanity. For instance, whenever I do something that might be considered clever, I try to take no notice whatsoever. Or if I must think about it, I look for flaws. *"Not* top quality work," I say to myself. And whenever I do something wrong I point it out to myself very firmly. "Anna," I say, "you are a perfect fool." I am not really sure that this is working.

How difficult it is being human! Inanimate objects never have all these complicated emotions. Just think how simple and pleasant it would be to go through life as an object. An attractive little blue sugar bowl with a painted bird on the lid, for instance, sitting in a patch of sunlight on the breakfast table. How peaceful, how tranquil, that must be. And if a careless elbow knocked you over and you smashed to bits, you wouldn't care, why should you? Being brainless has its advantages.

I love things; they are so patient and good. They'll

do anything you ask, anything at all, if only you understand their nature and treat them well. Things never make me nervous the way people do. Even *I* make myself nervous.

But back to the secret room. The library in our house shared a wall with the main staircase. It was a broad, impressive staircase with a curving mahogany banister, and underneath was a narrow, wedge-shaped cloakroom. Since this cloakroom tapered down to a point at the foot of the stairs, most of it went unused. There was a coat rack right by the door, with a jumble of hats and gloves and boots, but the dark recesses of the room were filled with nothing but dust and darkness.

I erected a thin plasterboard wall behind the coat rack. This gave me an enclosed area five feet by five feet with a steeply sloping roof. I carefully painted the new wall to look as though no wall was there; anyone pulling on a jacket or a pair of boots would see only the accustomed back of the closet, empty and dusty as usual.

The next step was a rather large-scale, noisy project. To distract my family's attention, I began work on a great number of repairs and improvements around the house all at once, at all hours of the day and night. I hammered and drilled and power-sanded here, there, and everywhere. I shut off the lights and water for hours and then turned them on again. I dismantled the bathroom sink and left it in pieces all over the upstairs hall.

The first few days, my family complained bitterly, shouting my name, banging on the pipes, and thumping on the ceiling with brooms. This was painful for me; angry people make my stomach hurt. However, gathering up my courage, I carried on. I took apart the table saw and brought it up from the basement. Then I reassembled it in the dining room and began cutting up a great stack of plywood.

This seemed to do the trick. They became resigned and lay on sofas in the front parlor with their heads wrapped in pillows, moaning softly. That was when I knew it was time to begin work in the library.

That night as they slept (or tried to), I erected a whole new wall in the library, parallel to the wall that backed on the cloakroom. The new wall was two feet closer to the center of the room than the old wall, leaving a narrow passage down the whole length of the room. I installed a trap door to the basement at one end of the passage, which gave me an entrance to my hidey-hole. No one but me ever goes down to the basement, so it would be much more secure than an entry on the first floor. Then I cut a door in the inner wall to connect the passage with the little chamber I had carved out of the cloakroom.

For those of you who are confused, or who skipped the last paragraph, feeling that it was too dull to follow, let me summarize: I now had a very small room under the stairs connected to a passageway through the library. This passageway could only be entered through the basement.

All that remained was to make the library look untouched. Working rapidly, I installed the built-in bookcases from the old wall onto the new wall and replaced the books in their proper order. Finally, as the sun rose in the eastern windows, I swept up the floor, re-laid the carpet, and put the furniture back in place. As I staggered off to sleep in the back of a clothes closet, I felt that I had put in a good night's work.

My family never noticed. There were so many rooms in that house, there simply wasn't time to sit in them all, let alone memorize their exact dimensions.

The next day I quickly finished up the various jobs I had begun all over the house and tidied things up again. My mother and sisters were cranky from lack of sleep and hot water, so I kept well out of their way. When everything was back to normal, I crept into my secret room. As it happened, my family chose to sit in the library (a favorite place for homework) that evening, and I found that I could hear them chatting and moving around the room with perfect clarity. Inside the wall I smiled. It was a small, secret smile; the smile of a snail curled up snug and safe in its shell.

It was pitch-black dark in there. I have good night vision, but it was too dark even for me, so I drilled tiny holes in the walls to let in some light. Later on, of course, I electrified my room, but back then I didn't mind the gloom. I didn't mean to live there, you see. All I wanted was a really secure hiding place.

And I had one. Was there ever such a wonderful little room! So long as I was enclosed in those four walls, I was strong and secure; I could do anything. No one could harm me, no one even knew where I was.

While I spent my time fitting out the room and making it comfortable, I could forget about the psychologist, about school, about the future. With much pushing and shoving, I managed to wrestle a big squashy armchair down to the basement and up through the trap door, down the passageway and into the room. Once I had added a footstool, a big cozy quilt, and a small but sturdy table, my little room was as neatly filled as an egg.

I spent as much time there as I could, contentedly sewing by candlelight. Often I would pause and look about me, smiling a little at my own world within the walls of my own beloved house. Some nights I even slept there, curled up in the quilt in the big old armchair.

In my room I almost felt that I had become a part of the house. I could hear its heartbeat, the rumble of its pipes, the creak of its timbers. Sometimes an overwhelming love for the house would well up inside of me so that I wanted to cry. It loved me too, I could tell.

We were necessary to each other; I protected it against the ravages of time and creeping dry-rot, and it sheltered me and gave me strength.

I loved it because it was strong, but I also loved it because it was blind and mute and deaf. It had no eyes to see me or ears to hear me or tongue to scold me. It did not judge me, it only held me close in its arms and rocked me gently to sleep through the long silent nights.

three

The day the psychologist was to come arrived.

"Anna, where are you?" my mother called, her voice sharp with anxiety. When I appeared she caught me by the arm and gripped me firmly, as though she thought I might run away.

"Now, Anna, I want you to stay right here where I can keep an eye on you. Sit in this chair by me . . . no, maybe you would be better off in the red chair. We want to get some contrast between you and your surroundings."

Unhappily I hoisted myself up onto the red armchair.

"Looks like somebody left an old dustrag lying around," Andrea observed critically. "Mrs. Waltzhammer'll think we think she's the new cleaning lady."

Both Mother and Kirsty turned on her.

"Don't you call Anna an old dustrag!" Kirsty shouted.

"Andrea! That will be quite enough out of you," said Mother sternly.

"You wait," Andrea said ominously. "You'll see. Mrs. Waltzhammer is going to wipe up the floor with her."

"Don't worry, Anna. *I'll* protect you," Kirsty said. "Nobody's going to use *my* sister for a dustrag," and she waved her fist belligerently at an imaginary Mrs. Waltzhammer. This encouraged me a little, but only a very little. I was stiff with terror.

"Maybe I should tie a ribbon in your hair," my mother worried. At that moment the doorbell rang. We all froze and stared at each other.

Mother recovered first. "Well," she said in an artificial voice, "that must be Mrs. Waltzhammer," and she hurried off to answer the door.

"Here," Kirsty whispered, thrusting her doll at me. "You can hold Bethany. Whenever I'm scared, Bethany makes me feel better."

I took Bethany onto my lap rather reluctantly. She was a large doll, really quite as large as I was. I couldn't help but feel that I must look a little foolish. Still, it was kindly meant, and I couldn't afford to reject any possible source of comfort.

We heard voices from the front hall. First Mother's voice and then another woman's voice, a powerful contralto that cut through walls like a chain saw. Kirsty glanced at me nervously. She looked as if she were about to ask for Bethany back.

Footsteps approached. The woman was talking, her words rolling and rumbling around the halls like boulders in a landslide.

"Great house!" she shouted. "I love these old houses! I'll bet the upkeep just about kills you, though, on a place this big."

"The girls help out, especially Anna. She's very talented that way," Mother said.

"Oh?"

"I know I shouldn't say so, Mrs. Waltzhammer, but Anna really is quite an exceptional child. In *many* ways."

Mother opened the door to the front parlor. "Mrs. Waltzhammer, I'd like you to meet my family," she said. "This is my eldest, Andrea, and my youngest, Kirsty. Kirsty will be starting at Bitter Creek Elementary this fall."

"Pleased to meet you," bellowed the woman. I cringed. Mrs. Waltzhammer was at least ten feet tall and six feet wide. She had an enormous bush of flaming red hair, and she carried the largest purse I had ever seen.

"And this, of course, is Anna. Right there on the red chair." Mother pointed helpfully.

Mrs. Waltzhammer rotated her huge body in my direction. "How do you do, Anna?" she boomed.

There was a moment's stunned silence.

"You mean . . . you can see her?" Andrea asked.

"Why, certainly," Mrs. Waltzhammer said.

"You don't think she looks like an old dustrag, do you?" Kirsty asked anxiously.

"Of course not. I think she looks like a very pretty little girl."

"Well, naturally!" Mother said, sounding relieved. She laughed a bit hysterically. "All my daughters are pretty. Now, if you'll excuse me, I think I hear the tea water boiling. Mrs. Waltzhammer, will you take coffee or tea?"

"Oh, coffee, coffee! Got to have my daily ration of caffeine," she roared with senseless laughter. "While you're gone I'll get a little better acquainted with your children." She winked at Mother, meaning, I suppose, that Mother should take her time bringing in the refreshments.

Mrs. Waltzhammer lowered herself into an armchair with considerable difficulty and then turned to Kirsty.

"So! I understand from your mother that you are a very shy young lady, Kirsty," she said, smiling genially.

Andrea snorted with laughter.

"No, no!" Kirsty said. "It's Anna who's shy!"

"Ah! It's *Anna* who's shy. I beg your pardon."

Mrs. Waltzhammer sat staring at me thoughtfully for a few moments. "Perhaps Anna would prefer it if I ask the two of you my questions and you can answer for her. Do you think that would make her more comfortable?"

"Yes, I think that's a great idea." Kirsty nodded her approval. I sighed with relief.

"Then tell me, if you would be so good, a little about your sister Anna."

Kirsty spoke up. She told Mrs. Waltzhammer the family legend of our father's shyness, and how much I resembled our father in that respect. Mrs. Waltzhammer seemed to be very interested in our father.

"Tragic," she said, shaking her head weightily over our father's fate. "A disappearance is so much harder on the family than a straightforward death or divorce." She sighed, a great gust of breath that stirred the uneven hem of my tunic. Still, large and noisy as she was, she seemed genuinely sympathetic. Cautiously I began to think that Mrs. Waltzhammer might not be the ogress of my nightmares.

Kirsty went on to tell Mrs. Waltzhammer how clever and hardworking I was. I stuck my fingers in my ears during this speech and murmured, "Exactly the reverse! Stupid and lazy, that's what you are!" to myself.

I unstuck my ears in time to hear Mrs. Waltzhammer say, "I'm sure she is, Kirsty. And she is your special friend, isn't she? More than say, Andrea's?" she smiled kindly at Andrea.

Kirsty nodded vigorously. "Yes, she is! Anna likes me much better than she does Andrea!"

"I *beg* your pardon," Andrea sputtered.

"You're mean to her," Kirsty shrilled. "You say awful things about her."

"I do not!"

"Well, no need to argue about it," Mrs. Waltzhammer said hastily. "Perhaps it's time for me to get to know Anna a little better." She rose from her seat and advanced on me.

Alarmed, I shrank back in my chair. Mrs. Waltzhammer opened her enormous purse and rummaged around in it. She drew out a pair of reading glasses and put them on, dropping the purse on the floor by my chair.

She smiled hugely at me, a jovial giantess.

"HELLO, ANNA!" she bawled. She reached out one vast white hand toward me. I stared in horrible fascination at the hand as it approached.

"What are you doing?" Andrea demanded in a strangled croak.

"Just saying hello to Anna," Mrs. Waltzhammer said in a jolly voice.

The hand gripped me insecurely about the waist, crushing me up against the doll. I was lifted up and —

My mind fell into darkness and I knew no more.

"That's not my sister, that's a *doll*," Kirsty was saying patiently when I came back to my senses again. She sounded as though she'd said it before.

I knew a moment of pure panic. I could hear Kirsty's voice, but I had no idea where I was. I seemed to be lying in a very small padded cell of some kind. I could see the ceiling of the front parlor above me, but all around were flabby, leathery walls. Underneath me were a lot of loose sharp objects that dug into my back.

"Well! Here I am at last!" It was my mother's voice. "This house is so big," she said gaily, "I guess I just got lost coming back from the kitchen!"

"Oh, coffee! Goody!" Mrs. Waltzhammer's voice was mercifully deadened by the walls of the padded cell, but she was standing dangerously near.

I heard sounds of slurping as Mrs. Waltzhammer imbibed her favorite beverage. "Good and strong," she exulted.

"And how have you all been getting along while I was doing the tea tray?" Mother asked.

Silence from Andrea and Kirsty.

"Excellently!" Mrs. Waltzhammer said. "I think we have made great progress. And now I'm afraid I must eat and run. I have another appointment. Delicious cookies, my dear."

"Thank you, but Anna made them."

Mrs. Waltzhammer's laugh rang out.

"Oh, *Anna* made them, did she? Clever, good Anna!" She laughed again. "Why don't you walk me to the door, Mrs. Newland?"

"Mom!" I heard Andrea's urgent whisper, "She thinks Anna is Kirsty's *doll!* And we can't find Anna."

"What, dear?" Mother murmured, but then a huge flap fell down over the top of my cell and the ceiling disappeared. The world lurched underneath me. A hail of large, angular objects fell about me. I reached out for something to hold onto, but there was nothing.

"Help," I cried. "Help!"

I thrashed about for a while, unable to get onto my knees. Outside there was a hearty booming that sounded like Mrs. Waltzhammer, and a worried tweeting that sounded like Mother. Thankfully, the movements stopped for a moment, and I struggled into a better position. Then, abruptly, off we went again.

This time, however, I had gotten my head out under the roof-flap and my knees were braced against some hard surface.

A mass of green shrubbery bobbed into my field of vision. I saw a concrete path below me and a green lawn. We were approaching a car parked by the side of the road. I looked up as best I could from under the flap. Far above floated Mrs. Waltzhammer's huge face.

I was in Mrs. Waltzhammer's purse. In a moment she would get into her car and we would drive away. In one convulsive movement I leaped clear of the enveloping purse and landed hard on the pavement.

There was no time to be lost. I scrambled painfully into the shrubbery. Mrs. Waltzhammer made a sound like, "Ugg-gugh!" It sounded like she'd swallowed her tongue. She looked furtively around and then hurried into her car and drove away.

I was out of the house.

For the first time in years and years, I was out of the house. I stood alone under the naked sky with nothing but air and space between me and the huge, barbarously bright sun. I looked up into the sky and grew dizzy. At any moment, I felt, I might fall off the earth, I might be pulled into the greedy heat of the sun. Or I might go flying off into dark, eternal nothingness.

Quickly I looked away, looked at the houses and trees and cars, trying to root myself to the ground. But everything was so far away! I had spent many hours lately inside the wall, and I had grown used to its proportions. Inside the wall all distances are small; all horizons are close at hand. It is easy to forget how large the world is, and how empty.

I bolted into the house, down the cellar steps, up through the trap door, and flung myself sobbing into my secret room. I wouldn't be leaving again in a hurry.

four

Five years went by.

I did leave my secret room, of course, but only when everyone was out, or by night after they were in bed. Otherwise I lived almost entirely inside the wall.

The night after Mrs. Waltzhammer came to visit I crept out and left a note:

> I'm sorry but I can't go to school.
> I really am very sorry.
> Please don't be angry with me.
> Anna

It did no good. Mother was furious.

She shouted and stamped her feet. She *demanded* that I come out and explain myself face-to-face. So, trembling like a blade of grass in a positive hurricane of indignation, I came out and stood before her. It didn't help. Nothing I could say would convince her that I hadn't hidden in Mrs. Waltzhammer's purse on purpose, in spite of Mother's express prohibition. I'm afraid I am not very good at explaining things, or arguing my point of view.

"In her *purse*, Anna! How could you! She might have carried you off with her!"

"I didn't mean —" I began.

"Anna, when I ask you a question I expect an answer. What would you have done if Mrs. Waltzhammer had walked right out of this house with you in her purse?"

"But she did!"

"Where are you now, Anna? Don't you be disappearing on me like that, young lady!"

"I'm right h —"

"And for another thing," Mother said, staring angrily at the draperies, where she apparently thought I was hiding, "Mrs. Waltzhammer must think I'm completely crazy, getting her here to talk about enrolling a doll in Bitter Creek Elementary School."

"Mrs. Waltzhammer doesn't think you're crazy, not really," Andrea said. "Just a little . . ." she groped for the word. "Over-tactful, I guess. She thinks it's Kirsty who's scared of going to kindergarten for the first time, not Anna." Mrs. Waltzhammer believed, Andrea said, that Kirsty was using her doll to express her anxieties over starting school. And that Mother and Andrea had simply gone a bit overboard in humoring her.

"If Mrs. Waltzhammer thinks anybody is nuts in this house it's Kirsty," Andrea concluded. Andrea, always the prettiest of the family, was beginning to show signs of being the cleverest as well.

This version of events did not please Kirsty, but did cheer Mother up some. In any case, Mrs. Waltzhammer only called back once. She told Mother to please contact her if either Kirsty or "Anna" had any problems in the fall and then hung up without waiting for an answer. The abrupt end to this call surprised Mother, but not me. I suspected that my exit from Mrs. Waltzhammer's purse had considerably unnerved her, and she wanted to have as little to do with the Newland family as possible.

The result of the whole Mrs. Waltzhammer episode was to make me much more secretive, much more secluded. It proved that my doubts and fears about the outside world were absolutely true. After all, the very first time I didn't hide myself away from an outsider, I was manhandled, kidnapped, and then abandoned. And that took place inside my own home, in front of my mother and sisters. Think what might happen if I ventured out into the wide world!

It seemed unreasonable to expect that, having regained safety entirely through my own efforts, I would consent to come out again. The crashing and booming of Mrs. Waltzhammer's voice mingled with my mother's angry voice in my mind's ear, and as time went on I burrowed deeper and deeper into the fabric of the house to escape from the memory.

Year after year I went on building, adding new passages, new secret rooms, until I could go almost anywhere in the house without coming out into the open. I installed a small but usable kitchen immediately behind the real kitchen. My cupboards were simply doors into the back walls of the real cupboards, so I had access to all the kitchen supplies. I had a stove (discarded by Mother and repaired by me) and a sink (a laundry tub rescued from the cellar), but no refrigerator, so when I needed milk or butter or eggs I had to creep out and get them without being noticed.

Over the years the rooms that Mother and Andrea and Kirsty lived in gradually dwindled and shrank. In one daring acquisition I walled off three entire rooms at the back of the house. They were part of the old servants' quarters and no one ever used them. My family never seemed to notice or care. It was a large house and they were not observant.

I installed peepholes in every room so that I could see as well as hear my family, placing them in dark corners and under picture frames so that the white of my eye would not gleam when I looked out. I tried to respect my family's privacy; I put no peepholes in the bathroom and rarely used the ones in their bedrooms. These holes gave me a disjointed, fragmentary view of my mother and sisters. Only occasionally did I see them in their entirety; more often they were represented by a hand, an elbow, the back of a head, sometimes a knee or a foot. I learned to read emotion in the lift of a wrist, the angle of a spine, the nervous twitch of an ankle.

Andrea, I think, almost forgot about me after a while. Although we shared the same initials and the same birthday, we had little in common. Indeed, we were almost opposites; it was as if she had somehow taken all my bloom and assurance for herself, leaving me pale and trembling.

In any case, she was busy with an intense emotional life of her own, quarrelling and making up with her girlfriends, and later, her boyfriends. Her angular dark looks bloomed into beauty at thirteen and she was suddenly in great demand. She spent her after-school hours in royal procession from the house of one friend to another. I saw her sometimes holding court on the front steps, a queen bee among a swarm of admirers. At first she rarely ever invited any of her friends inside. I liked to think that that was in deference to my feelings, but sometimes I wondered if, like our father, she was engaged in slowly disengaging herself from our family.

Eventually, though, as I faded more and more into the woodwork, she began to bring her friends home. The house thronged with groups of chattering teenagers. They surged in and out of the house like the tides. They laughed and played guitars and popped popcorn and argued endlessly amongst themselves.

By this time Mother had managed to get a job at the insurance company which allowed her to work from home in the afternoon, leaving the office for home at one o'clock every day. This meant that she could poke her head out of the library, which she had taken for her at-home office, every now and then to provide some sense of a restraining adult presence in the house.

"Not," as she said rather fretfully, "that I have the faintest idea what they're up to back there in the old servants' quarters. They could be making bombs, for all I know."

To be honest, once I got over the shock of having strangers in the house, I enjoyed having them there. It was interesting, trying to follow their loves and hates and jealousies, and I liked watching them devour the little treats I made for them. But it did mean that I became trapped within the walls, like a fly encased in amber. I could never come out into the house proper except during the small hours when everyone slept, for fear of running into a fledgling musical group in rehearsal, a mixed group of boys and girls painting their fingernails black, or a solitary fifteen-year-old sobbing her heart out alone on a staircase.

Even though Andrea herself never saw me anymore, she seemed at first to be afraid her friends might catch sight of me. Whenever she came into a room with them, she would peer anxiously into the dark corners and rummage among the couch cushions before she'd let them sit down. Perhaps she didn't want them to hurt me, but I think that maybe she was a little ashamed to have such an odd sister.

Silent and unseen I remained, and so I suppose at last I became for her a half-remembered family myth, a strange story that mustn't be told. And since she couldn't share the joke with her friends, she pushed me to the back of her mind and her life.

Mother and Kirsty, on the other hand, didn't give up hope for a long time that I might be coaxed out of hiding.

Kirsty laid little "Anna traps": a box propped up on a stick and baited with a cookie — often one I'd baked myself. It seemed rude to just take the cookie and go away, and even ruder to pretend I hadn't seen it. So I liked to leave something in its place, like a crocheted skirt for her doll Bethany, or a little jar of hard candies tied with a pretty ribbon.

She talked to me often and included me in her games.

"Let's play queens and kings, Anna. You be the queen," she would say, "Bethany can be the king. And I'll be the beautiful princess." Then, even though I never said a word, she would argue with my interpretation of the queen's role.

"Don't be silly, Anna," she'd say. "*Queens* don't do the dishes. The *servants* do the dishes."

In a way I became what Mrs. Waltzhammer had thought I was: Kirsty's imaginary friend.

Mother took a more straightforward approach.

"It's all right, Anna, you win," she said. "I won't make you go to school. You can come out now."

When I didn't come out, she said it again. Sometimes she said it in anger, sometimes in sorrow. But I didn't come out. I knew how much it mattered to her that others see me, so that they would believe in my existence. I remembered how angry she got when she believed that Mrs. Waltzhammer thought she was crazy. I couldn't trust her.

I tried hard to make up for my disobedience. I cooked and cleaned and sewed and kept the house in good repair. I often left them little presents that I had made: toys for Kirsty, a jewelry box of inlaid woods for Andrea, an intricately carved and painted necklace for Mother.

But I wouldn't come out.

Finally even Mother and Kirsty went for weeks at a time without speaking to me. When they did speak it was usually because they needed something. They began to forget that I was a real flesh-and-blood person; they confused me with the house itself. I didn't mind; I often thought of myself the same way. Every night Mother kissed her hand and pressed the kiss to the wall of whatever room she happened to be standing in at the time. "Goodnight, Anna," she would murmur, and then climb the stairs to bed.

Quite often I would be moving silently through my passageways and hear just the tag end of a whispered communication from Kirsty: ". . . and maroon satin on top. Don't you think that would look great, Anna? But don't bother if you don't have time. Thanks." Or Mother would say, ". . . fix the washer, Anna? I think it needs to be replaced." They thought of me, you see, as a kind of disembodied spirit, present and listening behind any wall of the house at any time.

I did try to honor these requests as best I could, but of course I often got things stupidly wrong, thinking that Kirsty wanted a ballgown for dress-up when what she actually wanted was a baseball jacket in the school colors. Or that Mother wanted me to put a new washer in the bathroom faucet when really it was the clothes washer that had stopped in mid-cycle and she wondered whether it should be repaired or replaced.

The other reason my family talked to me now and then was because I kept taking things and forgetting to return them. Even Andrea would mutter "Annadammit" under her breath and slap the wall with her hand whenever she missed something.

Well, I *needed* things. I naturally had a full set of sewing and carpentry tools inside the walls, but there are always times when you really, truly, have to have a nutcracker, for instance, or Volume II of the encyclopedia (AUST to BLIZZ). Or else sometimes I would start to mend something and get distracted halfway through. Then whatever the thing was would sit there in some dark corner until one of my family yelled for it. I might add that I often got the blame for taking things I had never touched.

It got pretty crowded in my rooms and passageways, to tell you the truth. I installed hooks and racks and shelves to keep things off the floor, but frankly, the dusting got to be kind of a nightmare.

Twice a year I did a major cleaning job. I put everything back in its proper place in the main house and swept and scrubbed the empty passageways. But you know how it is; you like a thing to be handy when you want it. Little by little one object and then another found its way back into my burrow. Two weeks after spring cleaning I'd be moving snakewise through the passageways again.

I was not entirely cut off from news of the great world. I saw snatches of television when I passed through the back parlor passageway and the set was on. It was never really comfortable watching it standing up, though, so I didn't make a habit of it. We also had a large library of books which I read and reread, and occasionally I rescued the odd magazine or newspaper before it was thrown out.

I even got some formal education, of sorts. Kirsty enjoyed playing school. She was always the teacher, and I was always the pupil. Besides delivering some rather silly lectures about a country she called Double

Pink Ponyland, and scolding me for imaginary misbe-havior, she insisted that I do the same homework that she did.

"I'm leaving my social studies and math books right here on the hall table, Anna," she would announce loudly. "Do the problems on page 169 and read Chapter Six."

I didn't want to hurt her feelings, so I did what she asked, even though the work was ridiculously easy. Sometimes I would see her studying my answers and then furtively changing her own paper to match mine.

Every once in a while I let Kirsty see me. It pleased her and did me no harm. I'd creep up behind her as she brushed her brown hair in the full-length mirror in the bathroom, and then slip away when she turned around. If she was sad, I would reach out and touch her hand. Kirsty hardly frightened me at all. I loved her.

In its way it was a good life.

But then I turned twelve.

five

That was a terrible time, the years between twelve and fourteen. I, who was never unwell, got sick. Or sort of sick; I was wounded in some mysterious way. I don't really want to go into the details of exactly what was wrong with me. It's kind of personal.

The, um, injury wasn't the only problem. I got two little pink bumps on my chest and hundreds of big red bumps on my face. I gained weight in unexpected places. Hair grew where no hair should grow. I —

Oh, never mind. I can't believe I'm telling you this. It's funny, you know? I feel that I can tell you, a perfect stranger, things I wouldn't dream of mentioning to Mother, or Kirsty, or Andrea. Or even my long-lost father. Or especially my long-lost father, come to think of it.

Perhaps I can talk to you like this because you can't see me or touch me or speak to me. You are like the house, that way. You listen without comment, or at least without any comment that *I* can hear. Whatever you may think of me, even if you think I'm a fool and a worm and a disgusting object, you can never, ever tell me so. I find that soothing in a confidante.

I didn't tell Mother about my troubles. If only it had been a less embarrassing affliction, I might have. I could have left a note, asking for advice. But these things were happening in the most private, secret parts of me, and I couldn't bear that she should know about it. I imagined her reading my note aloud to Kirsty and Andrea, and the shock and horror on their faces. No, I couldn't tell her.

Sometimes I thought I would probably die, and then again sometimes I thought that I probably wouldn't, and that almost frightened me more. Because you see, if I wasn't dying that meant I was changing, changing beyond any hope of recall.

I don't think I like change very much.

After a few months when I didn't die, I decided that I was being transformed into an altogether different kind of animal. In punishment for my eccentric lifestyle, I was turning into some sort of fat, hairy, bleeding monster with skin eruptions.

Accepting my doom, I began to stoop as I walked and let my hair fall over my face. I had always been fastidious in my hygiene, but now I washed myself less often so that I wouldn't have to witness any more changes in my body. And immediately my suspicions about my new nature were confirmed: when I didn't wash I smelled horrible. I smelled much worse, I mean, than I had before when I didn't wash. My perspiration now had a rank odor that appalled me.

I hung my head in shame and wished with all my heart that I could just peacefully pass out of life, that my flesh would wither away into air and darkness, and my bones become one with the bones of the house.

But that didn't happen. My thirteenth birthday came and went and I was still eating and drinking and breathing. In fact, I was eating like a horse. My appetite had always been delicate; I normally consumed less than a tenth of what Kirsty or Andrea or Mother did. Now I ate constantly, trying to dull the ache in my stomach.

Once or twice I tried to stop eating altogether, thinking that I could in this way put an end to my unhappy existence, but I always ended up in the main kitchen at two in the morning, steadily stuffing the leftovers from dinner into my mouth.

One night I caught a glimpse of myself reflected in the toaster. I had formed a habit whenever I passed the refrigerator of opening the door and staring moodily inside, and that was what I was doing now. I was gnawing ravenously on a cold chicken leg. My hair was matted and greasy. My skin was a flat, dingy gray with angry red pustules scattered across it. I had not changed or washed in a week or more.

It was true. I *had* become a monster, and a dirty, disgusting monster at that. If Andrea or any of her friends had seen me, if Mother or even Kirsty had seen me as I was now, they would have been horrified. They would have pointed at me and screamed in terror.

I stared at myself in the toaster. I straightened my back and pulled my hair out of my eyes.

Was I really a monster? Or was I just plain dirty? If I washed and combed my hair, cleaned the dirt out from under my nails, and changed into clean clothes, would I not be recognizably a human being? I thought that perhaps I would. Even though I knew that deep inside I had changed forever, maybe it didn't have to be so obvious.

I closed the refrigerator door and climbed up on the kitchen counter. I would take a bath right away and see. That was a problem, though. I was finding it harder and harder these days to squeeze myself into the kitchen sink.

Ever since I moved inside the wall, I had washed myself in the sink, either in the laundry tub on my side of the wall or in the main kitchen sink when the rest of the household had gone to bed. I couldn't use the bathtub because I had no entrance into the bathroom through the tiled walls. So once I got into the tub, I was trapped in the bathroom, naked and vulnerable. The kitchen sink, on the other hand, was right next to the broom closet, which led directly into my own kitchen on the other side of the wall.

But I didn't seem to fit in the kitchen sink anymore. My arms and legs hung out over the counter tops and my elbow kept getting in the way of the faucet. Even the laundry tub on my side of the wall was much too small.

I quickly found a solution. I took a shower instead. Standing up, I hosed myself down with the spray nozzle. This worked beautifully. I scrubbed and soaped myself all over, and soon I was pink and sweet smelling again. I trimmed and cleaned my nails. I massaged a little conditioning oil into my hair and, working patiently, combed out the knots. Then I climbed into a clean nightgown Kirsty had outgrown. All of my own clothes had shrunk mysteriously. They were painfully tight around the chest, and the bottoms of the leggings had climbed halfway up my shins.

Once again, I studied my reflection in the toaster. It was a little hard to see myself, but on the whole, I thought I looked more human than monstrous. In any case, I smelled much nicer. I resolved not to let myself get into such a state again. If I *was* a monster, I would be a clean, self-respecting monster.

The next day I began work on several new sets of clothes. Kirsty's nightgown was too big for me, of course, but not nearly as big as I would have expected. Evidently I had grown, which explained the difficulty I had been having recently in navigating through some of my narrower passages. I very much hoped that I wouldn't grow much more, or I'd soon be in serious trouble.

Once my new wardrobe was complete, I looked around myself for something else to do. During the whole of that dreadful time, I had sat sluggish and slothful, my hands idle in my lap. I had let things drift, and the house was beginning to show the signs of my neglect.

I had stopped baking and sewing. My workshop sat empty, gathering dust; I had only done repairs when absolutely necessary. No longer did I spend hours making mechanical toys for Kirsty or creating stylish hats for Mother or hand-painted vests for Andrea. I had withdrawn entirely from family life. I never watched them any more, or Andrea's friends either, although the walls vibrated with their music and hummed with their lives. All that had simply faded to noises heard from behind a wall, laughter from a party to which I had not been invited.

Now I stirred myself from my self-induced stupor. I whirled feverishly around my rooms and passageways, scrubbing, sweeping, dusting. When all was shiny and clean once again, I took stock of the house.

It was a positive shambles. The plumbing in the front bathroom had gone awry and needed immediate attention. An ice dam in the eaves last winter had caused a leak in a back bedroom, and the timbers of the house were quietly rotting inside the walls. The basement stairs had become rickety and dangerous, and the paint on the ceiling under the bathroom was peeling — an ominous sign. Clearly it was time that I stopped indulging my talent for self-pity.

My passageways were another concern. I had *not* stopped growing. On the contrary, I had to let out the seams of my first suit of new clothes while I was still working on the last. I could no longer reach the old servants' quarters because I couldn't, by any amount of squirming and wriggling, fit through the passageway that led to it.

Having strangers in the house was now a nuisance. The house was infested with Andrea's friends, from top to bottom, at all hours of the day and night. They seemed to be everywhere, in the laundry room, in the butler's pantry, in the conservatory. You never knew where they would turn up.

The girls among them had discovered a trunk of old turn-of-the-century clothes in one of the back bedrooms and had dragged it downstairs for dress-up. They took turns trying and failing to cram their huge feet and waists into the tiny shoes and gowns. When once they had managed to lace somebody up, they paraded through the house, shrieking with laughter and falling against each other. Kirsty, one of the few small enough to fit into the clothes, was allowed to join in. They dressed and petted her like a big doll, and she soaked up the attention like a sponge.

The boys mostly lay around on pillows grumbling about life. The only time they seemed to become animated was when Andrea entered the room. Then they'd sit up and begin arguing loudly amongst themselves and punching each other in a playful manner. When she left they would sink back on their pillows with a deep sigh.

"God, she's gorgeous," someone would remark, and they would all agree, nodding their heads fervently. Then they'd yawn and stretch and get back to the real business of their lives: complaining.

"My mother says I should get a job this summer instead of hanging around at Newlands' all the time," one would say gloomily.

"God," the others would groan, and stare bleakly at the ceiling.

Unfortunately, none of them could be relied upon to stay put. Even the boys bestirred themselves now and then in order to play their musical instruments or to dribble basketballs in the back hallways. And they weren't all alike, either. There were a few who roamed the house moodily by themselves. Two of the girls, for instance, seemed to have permanently broken hearts. They skulked around the servants' quarters, weeping furiously and muttering to themselves. And one of the boys, a short, rather chubby young man, spent all of his time alone in the front parlor playing scales on the piano. Whenever anybody looked into the room, he would stop abruptly and blush deeply.

How on earth I was going to get any work done around here was a mystery to me. And I was growing taller and bigger every day. Twice I got stuck in the bend of the passageway that led to the attic and had to spend several painful minutes unsticking myself. I began to carry a little jar of petroleum jelly around with me to help me through tight spots.

One thing, though. I was looking much better. I borrowed a hand mirror belonging to Andrea and had a good look at myself. I trimmed my hair and brushed it till it shone in the dim light. My skin was a little better now and my new shape no longer offended me so much. All in all, my reflection didn't look so bad. Perhaps, just perhaps, I was not a monster after all.

Suddenly I realized that it was August 18th. My fourteenth birthday was tomorrow. I smiled shyly at myself in the mirror.

Softly I sang:

> "Happy birthday to you,
> Happy birthday to you,
> Happy birth-day, dear Anna,
> Happy birthday to you."

Surely, I thought, I would stop growing soon. I would learn to live in my new body without shame. I would find a way to repair the house and enlarge my passages without being detected. Soon, very soon, everything would settle down and go along quietly in the old way.

six

I'm not a monster at all; I'm a woman.

Now I understand what has been happening to me
for the past two years. I was a girl, now I am a woman.
How simple, and how silly of me not to have realized.

After all, Andrea went through it before me. I ought
to have seen; I ought to have known. And now Kirsty
is on the same journey to adulthood. I have seen her
ruefully fingering a few skin blemishes, though neither
Andrea nor Kirsty seem to have suffered in this way as
much as I did. She stands sideways in front of the mirror in the hall, studying her chest. And sure enough,
there are two little bumps there. I'm glad to see her
pride in them. She seems to know what they mean and
to look forward with hope and pleasure. Mother probably explained it to her, as she would have done for me
if I'd only had the courage to ask.

In fact I have been surrounded for years by the evidence of adolescence. All those giggling, tearful teenagers I have watched through my peepholes; they

ought to have taught me something about my future. But somehow, your own story always seems unique, your own miseries unlike the miseries suffered by anyone else on the planet. It is hard to recognize your own particular predicament as the common fate of millions.

I am a woman. I am ridiculously proud of that fact, and yet — in a way it seems a little pointless. I'm assuming that all of these changes in my body mean that I am supposed to be involved in some sort of interaction with — well, with a man. But I am inside the wall. No men ever come here inside the wall, thank goodness, and I never go out.

So what good is it, being a woman in the wall?

There is a certain urgency to my question. I'm in love. Oh, I am in love!

I'm sorry. I had to stop for a brief fit of weeping. Falling in love seems to make you awfully moody. My emotions fly randomly from laughter to tears, like a little brown carpet moth caught up in the whirlwind of spring cleaning, fluttering now here, now there.

Would you like me to describe to you the man that I love? I can't! I know it sounds stupid, but I have no idea who he is. I've fallen in love with a cloud, a vapor, a nothingness. More specifically, I've fallen in love with a letter written on ivory notepaper in brownish ink, and with the mind and hand that wrote that letter.

There! You see? Now I'm laughing for no reason, except that thinking of him makes my heart lift in a strange way. I have to be careful, though. If one of Andrea's friends heard someone laughing to herself inside the wall, they might think it a bit peculiar.

When I first saw the letter, I was frightened. It was two days after my fourteenth birthday. I had gone to my little room under the stair to look for a lost tool (my Phillips head screwdriver; it's the only one I've got and I'm always losing it). I saw the letter at once, a little triangle of white like a spear point protruding into my private place. It had been folded over and over again into a tiny square. It was pushed into a narrow crack in the molding under the main staircase.

I stopped and stared. Nothing had entered my domain in all these years except those things that I brought here myself. Slowly I reached out a hand and touched the alien thing. I freed it from the crack in the wall and carefully unfolded it.

Dear A,
I love you.
Sincerely yours,
F

P.S. I'm too much of a coward to sign my name to this letter, or even to write yours. I know you'll never find this, but there's always the chance.

I dropped the paper on the floor and backed away from it as if it were a snake, smacking my head smartly on a stair tread. My heart thundered in my throat.

Someone knew I was here! I had been seen, observed! And by an outsider; no one in my family had that initial, "F." "A," of course, meant me, Anna.

But — what was that last sentence? I bent and picked up the letter gingerly between two fingers. "I know you'll never find this" must mean that the writer didn't know how close to the heart of my world he had come. The paper had been pushed through a random crack in the wall in hopes that I would come upon it by accident.

This calmed me somewhat. No one was going to come smashing through the walls of my sanctuary just yet. I studied the message carefully, with growing curiosity. I had never gotten a letter before.

"I love you," the paper said.

F didn't seem hostile, anyway. Far from it.

Who was F? What was F, a boy or a girl? A boy, I thought. I was pretty sure that girls didn't usually send love letters to other girls. Very well, I would assume that F was a he.

Apparently F had discovered my existence somehow, but I didn't think he could have seen me, and he had certainly never had any conversation with me. Was it possible to love someone, knowing so little about them? Now of course I realize how easily one may catch that particular disease, but back then I knew very little about the ways of love. The only love with which I was familiar was the love of my family, based on years of knowledge and familiarity.

I sat down in my easy chair and smoothed the letter in my lap. F, I mused. Who could F be? And should I (terrifying yet oddly exhilarating thought) answer his note?

Had I gone completely insane? Answer his note? I couldn't imagine myself doing such a thing. On the other hand . . . it wouldn't be as bad as actually speaking to a stranger, would it?

Mentally I began to compose a letter. "Dear Mr. F," I began, but then came to a halt. What could I say?

I could ask who he was, I thought. That seemed reasonable. How could he expect me to respond to his overtures when I didn't even know who was addressing me?

But it sounded as though he didn't want me to know his name. He said he was too much of a coward to sign his note in case I ever found it. Why should he be afraid of my knowing his name? My heart beat faster. I knew why. He was afraid because he was shy. He was like me.

It was astounding. F was worried about what *I* thought of *him!*

"Oh, F!" I breathed. "There's no need to be frightened of me. I know *exactly* how you feel. No one could understand you better, in fact!"

Poor F. Feeling the way he did, how courageous of

him to write at all! Of course I would answer his letter; it would be cruel not to. I would have to be careful what I said so that I didn't scare him any more than he already was. I folded his message and put it tenderly into one of my many pockets. Absently I picked up a scrap of linen on which I had been experimenting with embroidery motifs and began to sew, my mind busily considering my letter and a possible reply.

How would I deliver my response? I supposed I would have to use the same crack in the wall for a mail box. Well, then, I wouldn't sign my letter either. What if it fell into the wrong hands! It would be bad enough if my mother or sisters found it, but imagine if one of Andrea's friends, or Kirsty's for that matter, should find it? How they would scream with laughter! And the questions they would ask!

"Who is this Anna person?" they would want to know. It would put my family into an uncomfortable position.

What should I say? Not much, I decided. His letter had been short; so would mine be short. I wouldn't mention the part about his loving me. It was too embarrassing to discuss, when I knew so little about him. And I would only sign it "sincerely," instead of "sincerely yours" as he had; it would seem to be promising too much otherwise. But I must answer or else his feelings would be terribly hurt.

I looked down at my work and then laughed aloud,

very softly. Without really meaning to, I had already written my response. Neatly embroidered in gold on the white linen were these words:

> Dear F,
> I think you are *very* brave.
> Please, won't you tell me who you are?
> Sincerely,
> A

At least it was done, and done without too much heart burning. It looked rather pretty, too, surrounded with little embroidered flowers and vines in colored threads.

Quickly, without giving myself time to think about it, I hemmed up the little piece of material (it was only about five inches square), folded it up small, and pushed it firmly into the crack.

Then I went about my business. Or tried to. It seemed as though I could not get that little square of linen out of my mind. Whenever I was in a distant part of the house, I began to wonder if right *now* he was taking it out of the crack and reading it. Then I would hurry back to the room under the stairs, hoping to catch a glimpse of him.

Unfortunately, that crack in the wall had formed my only peephole into the whole hallway, and I couldn't see anything with the linen square blocking the way. I say unfortunately, but actually it was probably just as well. Otherwise I wouldn't have gotten anything else accomplished. I would have simply sat watching the hallway like a cat at a mouse hole, waiting for him to come and pick up his mail.

But he didn't pick up his mail. A day went by, and then a week. Then two weeks and three. I began to despair. The linen grew gray with dust. I cried sometimes, in the evenings.

I realized that I was becoming obsessed with this mysterious F. To keep my mind off him, I began work on a tailored tuxedo suit with satin accents on the lapels and pant legs for Andrea. I was absolutely determined not to look out my peepholes anymore or stare at that bit of dirty cloth stuck in the wall.

Being absolutely determined about something doesn't always give the results you might expect. Within an hour I heard a band of Andrea's friends coming up the kitchen stairway. I abandoned the tuxedo, which lay in pieces all over the floor of one of the back rooms I had annexed into my quarters. I hurried to the nearest peephole, tripping over the sewing kit in my hurry. Which? I wondered feverishly, which one was he? And why had he deserted me like this?

After that I simply abandoned myself to the mania. The tuxedo languished in a corner unfinished, the black satin spotted with my tears, the seams unsewn. I could think of nothing but F.

I had fallen in love like a stone falling into a well. His letter had released something in me, and now there was no going back. Once again I was changing, changing forever.

seven

Any dreams I had entertained of peace and normality were shattered now. I really think I went a little mad, those weeks after answering F's letter. It wasn't entirely the fault of the letter; I can see that now. It was those female chemicals percolating through my veins that were making me think new thoughts and dream strange dreams. F's letter did nothing more than explain my condition to me.

I was a woman because somewhere out there was F, a man.

I watched Andrea's friends through my peepholes, carefully studying all the body parts I could see. I thought to myself: that knobby knee protruding through ripped blue jeans could be *his* knee. Or that hand with the broad, flat thumb and bitten nails might be *his* hand. Is that the nape of his neck with the clipped blond hairs, or is it that one instead, covered by a mass of black curls? He had given me so little to go on, I found it difficult to imagine him.

It turned out to be difficult for me to tell Andrea's friends apart. I rarely saw them whole, and there seemed to be hundreds of them. To my inexperienced eyes they all had a certain resemblance to one another. Maddeningly, they traded clothing and accessories amongst themselves, so that a red sweater I had earmarked as belonging to a particular girl one day would show up on the back of a boy the next. Sometimes I felt like an animal behaviorist crouching on an ice floe trying to work out the social relationships of a tribe of penguins.

I was terribly afraid that F had stopped coming to the house anymore. Perhaps Andrea had quarrelled with him, I thought. She did quarrel with her friends quite often.

"Get out of here," I imagined Andrea saying to my poor, unfortunate F, tossing her long, glossy black hair contemptuously over her shoulder and pointing toward the door. "Leave, and don't come back."

Oh, Andrea!

Or had Mother frightened him off with one of her house-clearing sweeps? Mother was apt to wander through the house now and then, opening doors at random.

"Shoo!" she would say when she found some of Andrea's friends. "Go home! Go home and eat with your family. They haven't seen you in so long they've forgotten what you look like."

"Okay, Mrs. Newland," they'd answer in a mournful chorus, and then they'd gather up their shoes and socks and various other pieces of discarded clothing, their magazines, hair dye, book bags and stuffed animals, their guitars and amplifiers, drum sets and penny whistles and go, casting reproachful looks behind them. They didn't seem to take it personally, though, because so far as I could tell, the same ones would show up again the next day.

But F, I knew, was a more sensitive soul than the usual run of Andrea's friends. Perhaps Mother had singled him out for particular attention.

"You, F! [Fred? Felix? Ferdinand? What could his name be?]," she might have said, "Go home this minute! Your mother tells me she's going to report your disappearance to the Missing Persons Bureau."

And he, convinced that the FBI would shortly be on his track, had left, never to return. It seemed only too likely.

Even Kirsty might have insulted him somehow. Lately she had begun to toss her rather limp brown hair contemptuously over her shoulder and make rude remarks to people in faithful imitation of Andrea.

Tender-hearted Kirsty had shifted her sympathies almost entirely from the human race to the lower animals. She had become a vegetarian and was apt to be critical of the hamburger-devouring hordes around her. I could easily imagine her abusing my poor F for even looking at a baloney sandwich in her presence.

"Carnivore! Flesheater! Bloodsucker!"

No wonder he had fled from our house. I began to feel very sorry for F, and then for myself. How could my family be so heartless? My tears spilled out once again. As I sobbed, I reflected that if my life did not take a happier turn pretty soon, I would have to start including more fluids in my diet. The way things were going, I was likely to become dehydrated in no time.

For the first time in my life, I became restless, bored with the sameness of life behind the wall. I began to entertain crazy thoughts of leaving the wall, of going out into the world in search of F. But this was out of the question. Beyond the absurdity of my leaving this house, which had been a place of refuge all my life, how would I set about finding him? Ask every male I met: "Excuse me, sir, but would your name happen to begin with the letter F?" The whole idea was obviously ridiculous.

Yet something was stirring in me, something stronger than a whole lifetime of shyness. This longing had seized hold of me like a dog seizing a rat, and its grip did not slacken as the endless days went by with no word from F.

And then one day the crack was empty.

I stared, unbelieving. The cloth was gone. I searched carefully on the floor to make sure it hadn't fallen out, but no, the floor was bare. Then I began to worry that it had fallen the other way, onto the hall floor. I peered nervously out of the crack. No, I couldn't see anything, but it was hard to be sure.

Who had taken it, if anyone had? Maybe it had fallen out and been swept or vacuumed up. Maybe . . . maybe someone who wasn't F had found it and was even now entertaining a large group of rowdy teenagers with my little message. Or maybe it was F who was laughing over it now with his friends. Maybe F was just joking about loving me. Maybe F thought it was funny to write phony love letters to shy, inexperienced girls. Maybe . . .

I was a nervous wreck.

I twisted my hands wretchedly and tried to keep from making any sudden moves. These days, any impulsive movement was likely to result in bumps, bruises, and splinters.

I think you are very brave, I quoted to myself bitterly. How stupid! Why did I say such an idiotic thing?

Please, won't you tell me who you are? How prim and prissy I sounded. Andrea, for instance, would never have answered a love letter like that.

Andrea! How I wished I could have asked her for advice. She was so sophisticated, so knowledgeable about the world. She would have known exactly what to say.

I should have —

I heard a faint rasping sound. I whirled around and stared at the wall. It was back! Something had been pushed into the crack. I listened to footsteps, *his* footsteps, receding down the hall. If I had taken the letter immediately and peeked out, I might have seen him, but, frozen, I didn't move until all was silent again. Then I snatched it up.

It wasn't cloth. This was paper. I felt in the pocket where I always carried F's letter. It had become worn with reading and rereading by now. It was still there. This was another letter.

From F? I unfolded it. There was much more writing this time. I looked down at the signature.

F, it said, with a bold flourish.

"Oh!" I gasped in delight, and sank back in my chair to enjoy it.

This is what it said:

> Dear A,
> Omygod, A! I had no idea you'd ever find that letter. I just liked the idea of my letter being here in the walls of your house, crumbling away to bits, maybe, sixty years from now when you're an old woman and I'm an old man. Stupid, I know, but — I swear I never thought you'd find it. Here I am, babbling on. No, I'm sorry, I won't tell you who I am. I'm glad you think I'm brave, but I'm not. And if you knew who I was, you'd agree that cowardice is my

best policy when it comes to talking to a girl like you.

How smart and funny and clever of you to answer the way you did! In embroidery, I mean. It's the last thing I'd expect you to do. You are absolutely amazing.

Sincerely yours,

F

P.S. If the person reading this letter isn't A, I hope you burn in Hell for all eternity. Reading other people's mail is the act of a blob of pond scum.

P.P.S. I don't care who reads this letter, Andrea Megan Newland (See? I even know your middle name), I LOVE YOU.

I read this missive through and then read it once again; slowly, carefully, registering every comma and period, down to the last postscript.

He didn't love me. He had never loved me.

It was Andrea all along.

So. The obvious thing to do was to forward his entreaties to my all-conquering sister and then write back to him, telling him that his love letters had in fact been intercepted by a blob of pond scum.

It was the *right* thing to do.

But every time I thought of Andrea I felt a tight, burning sensation somewhere in my middle. At first I couldn't identify the feeling. It reminded me of images I had seen on TV, little drawings of the digestive tract showing acids churning around, eating holes in the stomach lining. Eventually it dawned on me that what I was feeling was anger.

Immediately I felt guilty. After all, Andrea probably had no idea of the pain she was inflicting. She wasn't doing anything but being herself. Was it Andrea's fault that F had fallen for her? No, of course not. It was *wrong* of me to feel anger toward her. And yet —

I thought of her, surrounded by admirers, and the bitter black bile climbed up my throat until I thought I would choke on it.

And F . . . I kept forgetting that it had always been Andrea he loved. There was nothing unfaithful or inconstant about his behavior; I hadn't been jilted at all. So, of course it wasn't his fault either. It was no one's fault but my own. I should have known that the letter wasn't for me. How could it have been? He'd never even known that I existed.

Stupid! I am so stupid!

Oh, F.

eight

Dear A,
Honest, I'd tell you my name if I could. Is that why you're not answering my letter? I've been checking every day.
Anxiously yours,
F

Dear A,
A?
Are you still there?
I promise I won't write your name out like that again for anybody to see. I realize that was an incredibly stupid thing to do and I'm really sorry. (Is that what you're upset about?)

Please answer this letter. I know you got the others because they were gone when I looked later.

Okay, so I'm acting like an idiot, but gimme a break, will you? I'm *grovelling* here.

Miserably yours,

F

It had been a week since I had received F's answer to my letter. I still had done nothing; I had taken no action at all.

Unfortunately, these last two letters did nothing to make him less attractive. On the contrary, he had begun to take shape as a human being, and now I liked him for his own sake, not just for his supposed passion for me.

He was shy, as I had thought, but his emotions were both strong and true. In fact, his last unhappy letter almost broke my heart. And that too was my fault. I was the reason he signed it "Miserably yours," not Andrea. He was suffering because of me.

Now, Anna, I said to myself sternly, stop behaving like a fool and a coward. Take a piece of paper and a pen and write the poor young man a letter explaining the mistake you made. Go on, do it.

Reluctantly I picked up pen and paper and began to write. But, I thought rebelliously, I *won't* give his letters to Andrea.

I signed my letter and read it over. To my dismay, I found that it wasn't at all the letter I had planned to write.

> Dear F,
> I'm sorry I haven't written. I have just a few questions:
>
> Do you like raisins?
> Do you have any food allergies?
> What is your neck size?
> How long is your arm? Please measure along your arm from the back of your neck to your wrist with your arm slightly bent.
> What is your favorite color?
> Are you dark or light?
>
> Thank you very much.
> Sincerely,
> A

I don't know how to tell you this.

I put that letter in the crack. I am deeply ashamed of myself, but that is what I did.

Oh, I made all sorts of excuses. My letter didn't actually claim to be from Andrea, for instance. Also, I would be much nicer to him than Andrea would be.

There was no denying that Andrea could be rather curt with her suitors, whereas I would shower him with loving kindness, raisin bran muffins, and exquisitely tailored shirts. I only wanted to make him happy. He would *be* happy too, believing that Andrea returned his love. And I — well, I, of course, would be in a state of ecstasy.

Naturally, though, none of these excuses were good enough. Assuming that I could convince him it was bright, beautiful Andrea writing to him instead of dull, plain Anna, wasn't that simply setting the stage for disaster? After receiving so much encouragement from Andrea (as he thought), wouldn't he someday be tempted to speak openly to her? Or what if instead he simply made some sly reference from our correspondence to the real Andrea, only to be met with blank incomprehension or ridicule?

No, the truth is that I was being selfish, plain and simple. If he thought I wasn't Andrea, he wouldn't answer my letter, so I allowed him to think I *was* Andrea. I simply couldn't bear to lose all contact with him. And I couldn't bear for him to think of me as a blob of pond scum, even though that is what I truly am.

After I left the note, I went away and stayed in the back of the house for the rest of the day. When I came back the next morning, I was disappointed to see that the letter was still there. Wistfully I pulled it out to reread it.

"Dear A," (it began).

It was from F, and it was two pages long! He had taken my letter, read it, and responded. With trembling hands I flattened it out and read:

> Dear A,
> Hmmmmmm. Well, okay . . . here goes.
>
> 1. Yes, I like raisins. Basically, I like food.
>
> 2. No, I have no food allergies. Otherwise, I am allergic to wool and some kind of detergent my mom used one time a few weeks ago to wash the laundry.
>
> 3. 5-inch neck (approximately — it's hard to tell where to start and stop measuring). My ears are each three inches long. I only mention it because this seems to be the kind of information you want. My nose is two inches long.
>
> 4. 32-inch arm. I had to ask my father for help with this. He thinks I'm nuts, but then he thought that

anyway. I'm not sure which arm you are particularly interested in, so I'll throw in the measurements for both. They're the same.

5. When I was a kid I used to love blue. I still do, but now I think my favorite color is brown.

6. This is a great question. Am I dark or light? I assume you are referring to my spiritual orientation, right? I would love to say dark — it sounds so much more interesting. Compared to most people, I probably am on the dark side. But I guess I'm both dark and light. Come to think of it, it's the contrast between light and shadow that's interesting, isn't it?
On the other hand, this may be a fishing question about my physical appearance. Since I am so grateful to you for answering my letters (at last!), I'll tell you. I am dark. My dad says we have some American Indian and Italian blood on his side of the family. So yes, I'm dark skinned and dark eyed.

If you don't mind my saying so, this is a very weird game you're playing. Do you really think you can guess my identity this way? The only question that might have been useful was the last one.

I'm not complaining, you understand. I'm amazed. You are so much more interesting than I thought. Not that I didn't think you were interesting before, because boy, did I! No, but there's a whole other part of your personality I never imagined.

If there are any more measurements or food preferences you would like to know about, let me know. In any case, PLEASE ANSWER THIS LETTER RIGHT AWAY IF NOT SOONER!

Yours (but holding a large butterfly net carefully concealed behind my back in case you try something funny),

F

P.S. I have a question of my own. What do you think of Mr. Albright?

What a wealth of information there was in that letter! Some of it I simply didn't understand (what, for instance, did he mean by the concealed butterfly net in his closing?), but overall I was delighted with my letter.

When I first read it, I thought I had a foolproof clue to his identity. I also thought I understood his reluctance to speak to Andrea in person. It was certainly going to be a challenge sewing him a dress shirt, though. Frankly, anybody with a neck that only measures five inches around is practically a freak of nature. Talk about a pencil neck! What size did he take in hats, I wondered? And how did he swallow his food?

Thinking things over, though, I decided that he had misinterpreted my request. He might have measured the *length* of his neck. Knowing nothing about sewing, he probably didn't understand which measurements were necessary. That would also explain his offering measurements of his ears and nose. And, of course, I never actually told him that I planned to sew him a shirt.

I was pleased to see him so open-minded about food. While I pride myself on pleasing the fussiest of appetites, there is no doubt that food allergies and aversions place obstacles in the way of the creative chef. It did look as if my half-formed plan to knit him a sweater would have to be cancelled, however, since he couldn't wear wool.

The letter also gave me plenty of hints about his personality and situation in life. His family, I saw, contained at least three people: his mother, his father, and himself. They seemed fond of him, too: his mother washed F's laundry, even though with inappropriate laundry detergents (which brand, I wondered?), and his father measured F's arms when requested to do so, even while expressing doubts as to F's sanity.

I sighed. Lucky F, to have a father actually in the house rather than lost forever in the storage stacks of the Library of Congress.

The introduction of this Mr. Albright struck a somewhat unsettling note. Perhaps he was a teacher? The name sounded faintly familiar; I was sure I'd heard it mentioned recently. The first name, I thought, was Frank. But what role Mr. Frank Albright might play in Andrea's life I could not imagine.

Remembering the request for a prompt response, I dashed off a quick note:

> Dear F,
> Tell me, how do you feel about coconut? Personally, I don't like it very much, but I know that many people enjoy it.
> I found everything you had to say in your letter very interesting, especially about your "spiritual orienta-

tion," as you call it. I guess I'd have to say that my spirit is more dark than light. In fact, sometimes I feel that the dark is my only friend.

I hate to bother you, but could you please measure your neck again? This time measure *around* your neck instead of up and down. Thank you. I really appreciate it.

Sincerely,

A

I decided not to say anything about this Mr. Albright. I might guess wrong and give everything away. With any luck F would forget his question.

After posting the note, I did a quick carpentry job on the hall closet. I fixed the shelf on the back wall onto a central pivot so that it could be rotated like a lazy Susan, facing either into my secret room or into the closet. I installed a sturdy latch on my side so that no one would ever accidentally knock it ajar and discover my private place.

The crack was all very well as a mail box for letters, but objects could never be exchanged through it. My new revolving shelf would give me a way to deliver the gifts I planned to make for F in perfect safety. Still, standing there admiring my workmanship once it was completed, I experienced a momentary qualm, a feeling not unlike a cold draft blowing at the nape of my neck. The revolving shelf was a door from the heart of my home into the outside world. And latch or no latch, that door swung both ways.

Impatiently I dismissed my fears, squeezed myself up through the passageway into the attic, and settled down to a leisurely examination of my sewing materials. I stroked the fabrics meditatively as I watched the sun set over the town through the dusty attic windows.

Reviewing my supply of magazines and clothing store ads from the newspapers, I realized that Andrea's male friends never seemed to wear dress shirts or three-piece suits. Usually they wore a tee shirt with some sort of advertising logo on the front. This offered no scope for my abilities at all.

What should I make for him? A plaid flannel shirt or a denim jacket with rivets? Perhaps a hand-painted tee shirt? I pondered my options one by one, taking up first one idea and then another, like a woman fingering the ornaments in her jewelry chest. It seemed to me at that moment that life could offer no greater luxury than this: the pleasure of slowly turning over in my mind *which* gift I would make for him first.

Never in my life had I been happier, or my hopes for the future brighter.

nine

Dear A,

What do you mean by saying that
sometimes you feel that the dark
is your only friend and then asking
me to measure *around* my neck?
You are beginning to make me
very nervous, lady. And what's all
this jazz about coconut? I hate
coconut. I loathe and despise coconut. It's the only food besides
lima beans and liver that I don't
like. I guess that's something else we
have in common besides our dark
souls.

Funny. You always seemed like
such a *normal* person before. Not
normal/ordinary, but normal/non-
peculiar. I mean, *I'm* supposed to be

weird, but boy have you ever got me beat!

Apprehensively yours,

F

P.S. Much against my better judgment I measured my neck. 15 inches.

Oh, dear. F was getting suspicious. I'd better sit down and write him an Andrea-type letter instead of an Anna-type letter. Well, what would Andrea be likely to write to F about? What *do* people talk about, especially when they don't know each other well?

Not only was Andrea beautiful, she was clever, which made everything more difficult. I too was clever in my way, but my way was not Andrea's way. I was clever with things, while Andrea was clever with people. And vice versa: I was stupid about people, while Andrea was downright half-witted about things.

I have evolved two strategies for dealing with people. First, I hide from them. Then, if that doesn't work, I try to pacify them with presents. Even I am beginning to see that my tactics are a somewhat inadequate response to the problem of interacting with other human beings.

But look at Andrea! If an inanimate object doesn't live up to Andrea's expectations, her reactions are even less sophisticated: She kicks it, curses it, and discards it. Then she nags Mother into buying a new one.

I didn't answer F's latest letter immediately. While I sewed him a brown western shirt with blue piping, I listened carefully to the conversations of the teens on the other side of the wall, trying to decide what I could write that would make me sound normal/non-peculiar, without sounding normal/ordinary, or worse yet, abnormal/peculiar.

After much thought and observation, I wrote this letter:

> Dear F,
> Just a few things I thought you'd be interested in knowing:
>
> 1. The lead guitarist of the Stinking Lemons lives exclusively on a diet of grape Kool-Aid, strawberry Twizzlers, and Hostess Cakes.
>
> 2. The economics midterm was murder.
>
> 3. The new Treat Williams movie is really stupid.
>
> 4. Kyle Winterbottom split his head open playing soccer yesterday. He was practically leaking brains all the way back to his locker, and nobody

did anything about it. His parents are probably going to sue.

5. Mia was grounded for a whole month just for talking back to her mother. Can you believe it?

6. A girl with pink plastic barrettes in her hair, whose name might be Kendra or else Tendra, is in love with a boy in an orange baseball cap, but he doesn't know it yet.
Sincerely yours,
A

P.S. Look on the shelf in the hall closet (under the main staircase).

I was very proud of number 6. It was the only piece of information I had found out for myself instead of simply overhearing.

The postscript, of course, referred to the fact that I planned to put the now-completed western shirt and a box of oatmeal raisin cookies on the shelf for him to find.

I enjoyed writing this letter. It made me feel like any normal teen-ager talking, or at least writing, to her boyfriend. *I can do it too!* I thought exultingly. *I'm not a freak!*

So I was a little downcast at first when I got his reply.

> Dear A,
> Okay, okay, I get your point.
> I'll admit I didn't at first. I thought, what *is* this peculiar letter? Can this really be the A that I know and love so well, writing this gibberish? Or is some wacko purloining my mail?
> But then I figured it out. You're right. That *is* the kind of stuff everybody always talks about. And it's boring. And I don't want to talk about it either.
> Although it is kind of interesting about Kendra and Steve.
> Tell me something. Why do you people keep oatmeal cookies in a coat closet? By any chance, did you mean those cookies to be for me? To eat? I sure hope so, because I did.
> Besides being delicious, they were very reassuring. I have this recurring nightmare in which somebody like Tiffany Jacobs stands up in the middle of assembly at school and starts reading this correspondence

out loud. Tiffany Jacobs would *never* bake me cookies, so you see, she can't possibly be the one writing to me.

By the way, I hate to criticize your choice of friends, but c'mon, A, Tiffany Jacobs?

Actually, it seems pretty incredible that you would bake me cookies either. I hope you don't think you've guessed who I am and got it wrong. I am *not* Foster Addams, for instance. Sorry, but I'm afraid I'm nothing at all like Foster Addams. By the way, I think he's kind of a jerk, don't you? Or don't you? Sometimes you act like you really like him.

Love,

F

P.S. There was a brand-new shirt all wrapped up in red satin ribbons underneath the cookies. Did somebody in your family misplace a birthday present?

P.P.S. You never said what you thought of Mr. Albright. I mean,

isn't he dating your mother? I heard
they're getting kind of serious.

I smiled and sighed over the first nine-tenths of F's
letter. How stupid of me not to put a note with the
shirt! And then I read the post-postscript. My disap-
pointment about the shirt and my failure at writing an
Andrea-type letter instead of an Anna-type letter evap-
orated instantly.

Chasms gaped beneath my feet. *What?* What did he
mean? How could this Mr. Albright possibly be "dating" my mother? And what did that ominous phrase
"getting kind of serious" mean?

At first, naturally, I assumed that it was some sort of
a sick joke, or possibly the result of a fleeting bout of
insanity on F's part. But with dawning horror I realized that this nightmarish notion might quite possibly
be true. Strictly speaking, the law maintained that my
mother was a widow. For her to go out on a date with
another man was probably not actually illegal. Broad-
minded people might not even consider it immoral.

But — but how could she be so cruel? Why, for all
she knew, my father might quite easily still be alive.
How would he feel if he came back after all these years
only to find my mother consorting with strange men?
The very idea was unthinkable. Why hadn't I known
about this before?

Forgetting F entirely, I hurried to my peephole into

the library, the room my mother used for an office. I ducked my head down, screwed up one eye, and peered through. My jaw dropped. There *was* a man in there with her. He was leaning back in a chair, *my father's chair*, and smirking in a truly horrible way at my mother.

After a few moments, I straightened up and massaged the small of my back with my thumbs. Well, that was one explanation of why I hadn't been aware of this Mr. Albright situation before. I had to twist myself up like a pretzel these days in order to get my eye down to the library peephole.

I strained my ears to hear their conversation. Unfortunately they were sitting at the far end of the library, which was a large room. The shelves of books and the heavy brocade curtains and massive Victorian furniture deadened the sound so that at first I heard only scraps and tag ends of their talk.

". . . dinner and a movie tonight, Elaine?"

So it was true. Elaine was my mother's first name. How dare he?

My mother murmured something in reply. It must have been a refusal, since he began to argue.

". . . surely they're old enough! Just put your foot down. You're a slave to your children, Elaine."

I bent again and squinted at my mother's face. She was weakening, I could tell. No, Mother, I thought, don't do it. Remember your wedding vows.

". . . don't understand," she said, her voice strengthening. "I know it's idiotic and irrational of me, but I can't help feeling that if I go out frivolling with you, Frank, I'll be punished for it. I have this image in my mind of the whole place going up in flames with my daughters inside, the minute I step outside the front door."

He made a rude noise. "That *is* idiotic and irrational. But if it would get you out of here now and then, I'd be happy to bring the kids along."

She shook her head, smiling. "Irrational fears aren't calmed by rational solutions, Frank. But," she hesitated and her voice dropped, ". . . admit I would enjoy it."

"Of course you would," he said briskly. Then, "Have you given any more thought to my other suggestion?"

"No." My mother's voice came through strong and clear. "No, Frank, if our getting married means my selling the house and leaving Bitter Creek, I can't do it, and I can't tell you why. I'm sorry; I don't mean to make a mystery of it, but I just can't."

Married! Selling the house!

I straightened up so abruptly that I hit my head against a wall stud with an audible *crack!* I groaned aloud.

"What was that?" The man's voice was suddenly much closer to me.

"Nothing!" My mother's voice was also much closer. "I didn't hear a thing!"

I reeled in agony and clutched at my head.

"If you didn't hear anything, why are you shouting like that?"

"I am not shouting!"

They were standing inches away from me. I held my breath.

"Relax, darling. It's only a mouse or something behind the books. Here, I'll just —"

"Get away from that wall, Frank!"

"Elaine, what on earth —?"

"Put those books back on the shelf," my mother said in a voice of steel.

"Very well." Mr. Albright's voice was cold as well.

I smiled through my tears. They were quarrelling. All was not lost.

"I wish I knew what put you into such a panic, Elaine," Mr. Albright said grumpily. "You are — very odd about this house. And this, as I've said before and will no doubt say again, is an odd house. *Very* odd, in fact."

Mother was silent for a moment. Then she sighed deeply and said, "I'm sorry, Frank. I'm all on edge today. I'm sure you're right; it's nothing more than a mouse inside the walls."

"Well, for goodness' sake, woman, don't sound so tragic about it. We'll put down some poison and get rid of it."

"No!" she said sharply. "No, I don't want to do that, just in case."

"Just in case what?"

"Nothing. I'm sorry, Frank, I really am. About everything." Her voice faded out on 'everything,' and I concluded that she had left the room.

"Elaine?" he called after her, his voice sounding a little forlorn.

Ha! Let him suffer.

"We'll have dinner." Her voice came back to us from afar. "Wait while I dress."

I gnashed my teeth.

"Elaine?" he called. After several moments went by without a response, I heard him fling himself into an armchair, making a disgruntled noise that sounded something like a cross between gargling and growling.

"Aarrghh!"

I leaned back down and peered through my peep-hole. He was back sitting in my father's chair again. And as if in mimicry of my poor vanished father, he had barricaded himself behind a newspaper.

I crouched there staring at him, unblinking, until my eye teared with the strain and my limbs stiffened and creaked. I didn't care; I didn't feel it. A murderous rage sang in my blood and roared in my ears. I knew at last what it was to hate without fear or restraint.

ten

So *this* was what had been brewing behind my back. How deceitful my family was, how sly!

They must, each and every one of them, be aware of this . . . this conspiracy. If F, a mere visitor to the house, knew, my sisters must. When F said that Mother and Mr. Albright were getting serious, he meant that they were thinking of getting married.

And no one else had thought to mention it to me. I could not imagine a situation that more directly threatened my happiness and security. My mother feared my death by fire; how much more merciful that would be than this!

The fact that my mother had refused so firmly did not comfort me very much. I saw how quickly she gave in about going out to dinner and a movie with this interloper. How much longer would she hold out against marriage? She was saying no now; would she still be saying no tomorrow?

And there was something else about my mother's

manner that disturbed me. When she agreed with Mr. Albright that the noise they had heard was nothing more than a mouse in the walls, she sounded like she meant it. Yet she must have known it was me; that was why she tried to steer Mr. Albright away from the walls and denied that there was anything to hear.

So why did she sound so sad when she finally conceded that my involuntary cry was only a rodent squeaking? And what did she mean by refusing to put down poison "just in case"? Just in case I was still here and might eat it by mistake? Why on earth *wouldn't* I still be here? Where else could I be?

I felt more and more uneasy as I thought about it. She had wasted no time in having my father presumed dead as soon as the law allowed. Just because no one had laid eyes on him for seven years, Mother and the District of Columbia, where he had disappeared, had been prepared to scratch him off the list of the living. That apparently put an end to any obligation Mother felt toward her husband. After all, here she was, a bare eleven years after his disappearance, being wined and dined by other men and listening to their marriage proposals.

I began gnawing nervously at my fingernails with my teeth. How many years did New York State require to elapse before death could be presumed? Would it be a longer or shorter time than Washington, D.C., I wondered? We had a book that would tell me, but it was on the library shelf, and that awful man was still in there.

I would have to wait him out. I climbed into my armchair and wrapped the quilt tightly around my body until I resembled a butterfly's cocoon. How long, I asked myself with rising dread, had it been since anyone had last seen *me?*

Five years. That was all the time New York deemed necessary before death could be presumed.

The hateful man and my mother had gone out together alone and unchaperoned to eat, drink, and be merry, leaving me to read the law and reflect upon my fate.

After five measly little years of non-appearance, the good people of New York State would decide you were no longer among the living and issue a death certificate with your name on it. The legal system seemed to me to be positively panting for the opportunity to start shovelling dirt onto your grave.

Let this be a warning to you not to retire to the privacy of your room for a spell of meditation and self-communion, or the next thing you know you'll be reading your obituary in the newspaper.

My mother and my oldest sister had not seen me for seven years.

Kirsty had seen me now and then, but not for at

least three years. All of those sightings were extremely brief, and none occurred after she was over nine years old. Would the law take the word of a twelve-year-old who wasn't really sure but who thought she *might* have seen her sister out of the corner of her eye three years ago?

The book in which I read about presumption of death also volunteered the information that a diligent search must be made for the missing person before he or she can be declared deceased. I tried to imagine what it would be like, being diligently sought after by the authorities.

I squeezed my eyes shut and curled up into a ball, whimpering softly to myself.

They would tear down my walls and lay bare my secret life.

Of course they would. My family might not be certain, but they must suspect that I had retreated into the walls, and they would tell that to the people who came to look for me.

The authorities, whom I now pictured as large beefy men with tattoos, leather jackets, and chains, could not possibly fit into my passageways, the big apes, even if they could find the entrance. No, they would have to smash their way in. They'd come after me with sledgehammers and crowbars and great, gleaming axes.

After a few moments of whining, snivelling panic, I regained control. Stop it, I commanded myself. Don't be ridiculous! Maybe my family hadn't been seeing much of me recently, but they had plenty of evidence of my presence, didn't they? Think of all the things I did for them: the snacks prepared, the clothing sewed, the repairs made to our mutual home.

But then I thought uncomfortably of how little I had been doing for the last few years. Immediately after the onset of adolescence, I was too depressed to do anything but feel sorry for myself and then, once I snapped out of my dejection, the house was too full of Andrea's friends for me to make much progress on repairs.

Frantically I tried to recall something, anything I had done lately that would prove my existence. Nothing. There was nothing. I had been angry with my family, believing that they had chased F away. The tuxedo I started for Andrea lay in ruins in a corner. The only gifts I had made for anyone in years were the cookies and western shirt presented to F.

F! F could tell them I was here! F could . . .

No, he couldn't. F thought I was Andrea.

I burst into tears. At first, out of force of habit, I wept silently, but then, in the extremity of my misery, I began to sob aloud, then to wail, a thin, keening sound like the wind in the chimney. What did I care who heard me? They didn't even believe that I existed anymore.

Even if my family didn't get the authorities to tear

down my walls, they were going to move away and leave me. Mother would marry that Frank Albright. And then they would SELL THE HOUSE. With me in it.

Such a horrible possibility had never occurred to me before. I knew, of course, that people did buy and sell houses. After all, Father had bought this house before I was born (no doubt the reason why the terrible Mr. Albright wanted to remove my mother from it). But it had never occurred to me that anyone in the family would consider *selling* our home.

What would I do if they did? I would be alone in the world. Even worse, I *wouldn't* be alone; I would have a whole new set of people moving in. I wept louder. I wanted my own people — Mother and Andrea and Kirsty — not some alien family with whom I had nothing in common.

And F. I would certainly lose him as well. The new family probably wouldn't even be acquainted with him; they'd never ask him to visit. I would be cut off from everyone and everything I held dear.

Then there was the fact that I had, over the years, taken over so much of the house. The new people might notice that the interior dimensions of the house did not match the exterior dimensions and decide to investigate. When they realized that nearly half the square footage of the building was inaccessible to them, they might quite reasonably resent the fact.

And they probably wouldn't much care for my eating their food. My appetite was still unfortunately rather hearty. Unless they had numerous children or flocks of visitors (as we had), they would be bound to realize before long that someone else was sharing the groceries. Or unless I went on a rather drastic diet. I sighed. *That* wouldn't last long. I was feeling rather empty right now.

So it amounted to this: even if the State of New York didn't try to hunt me down, once the new owners found that they had an unwelcome guest, they would probably hire an exterminator to evict me. One morning I would wake up dead; gassed, trapped, poisoned, I would be entombed within the walls. And who would there be to grieve for me?

At this pathetic picture I howled aloud with rage and self-pity. I flung myself down on the floor and drummed my heels against the walls of the house, careless of who might hear. I *wanted* them to hear. I wanted them to know that I, Anna, was taking this very personally. How *dare* they treat me like this? After everything I'd done for them!

"I hate you!" I shouted at the top of my lungs, "I hate all of you! Selfish *pigs!*" I shrieked. I screamed every insult I could think of until the words began to run together. Finally the power of speech failed me and I simply howled. There seemed to be an almost limitless fund of fury in me; more anger than one would think that a small person like myself could possibly hold. It came streaming out of me in a steady, hot ribbon of sound.

After a time I quieted a little. For one thing, with all this uninhibited thrashing around, I was a mass of slivers, bumps, and bruises. My head throbbed. It was still sore from where I had banged it earlier as well as from emotion. I ached in every joint. Life between the walls didn't afford enough space for this sort of behavior.

Great shuddering sobs convulsed my body, and the floor became wet with tears, but I stopped shouting and kicking. I felt tired and ill, as though I was coming down with the flu. Gradually my crying slowed; my chest stopped heaving, my breath stilled. My nose was completely stuffed up, but I had neither the energy to blow it nor the handkerchief to blow it on. I closed my hot, swollen eyelids and, breathing noisily through my mouth, lay inert for a long time, not thinking, not moving. Very slowly I drifted off into an exhausted slumber.

I slept. And as I slept I dreamt that the house was on fire.

In my dream, I awakened into a queer yellowish-gray half-light. The air around me was thick and heavy and bitter to taste. When I gasped for breath, I began coughing weakly. I tried to get up but fell back again, dizzy and nauseous. *What's the matter with you, Anna?* I scolded myself, and with an enormous effort of will, I sat up. The murky air swirled thickly about me. Far off I heard a vast roaring, sucking sound.

Suddenly I was standing, not in any of my passageways or rooms, but in the main entrance hall of the house. The great oak doors were thrown wide open, and out on the lawn stood a great crowd of people. I saw Kirsty and Mother, and Andrea with a flock of friends clustering about her. Mrs. Waltzhammer was there, and Mr. Albright and all the neighbors. And there — that sad, gray man lurking behind the lilac bush — wasn't that my father? And F. His features were hazy, but I knew instinctively that that was F smiling and beckoning to me.

Anna! I knew it was F speaking, though I had never heard his voice before.

Anna! Kirsty was calling me now, with love and anxiety in her voice. *Anna, come out! The house is on fire!*

I turned around to look behind me and stared into the face of an inferno. It was white-hot and ravenous, like the hungry sun I had glimpsed from under the shrubbery all those years ago. I put up a hand to shield my face. I could see nothing but a blinding radiance.

I whimpered in my sleep and woke with my heart thumping in my ears. The blinding light was still there.

And so was someone else.

Someone was behind the light, someone was *here* inside my secret room. I could hear the rasp of labored breathing, the floors and walls creaking with an unac-customed bulk. I could *smell* an alien presence: some sort of deodorant or shampoo, I suppose.

"Hello?" said a voice, shockingly close at hand.

I felt the hair on the back of my neck stand straight up and my body temperature plummet by five degrees.

"Hello?" said the voice behind the light. "Is that you, A?"

eleven

I froze. I did not move a muscle. If I simply lay perfectly still, the person would never see me.

"Well," the voice said impatiently, "answer the question, can't you? Don't just lie there with your jaw hanging open. It's not particularly attractive, you know."

It was true, I did have my mouth open. He saw me!

"Are you A or not?" the voice persisted.

I found my voice. "Not," I whispered.

"What?" it said irritably. "Speak up."

"N-not," I repeated, louder this time.

This did not pacify the voice.

"Don't give me that 'not' stuff," it said. "Sure you are. You must be A. Who else? I mean, there isn't anybody else living in here, is there?"

I shook my head no. What a fool! I should have said that there was a whole colony of us living inside the wall and all of us, to a woman, armed to the teeth.

"Were you the one having the temper tantrum?"

I sat up abruptly. "What do you mean, 'temper

tantrum'?" I asked, offended. Kirsty used to have temper tantrums for years, up until she was about seven years old. I had always found them deeply embarrassing to witness.

"The usual, I guess," said the voice, sounding perplexed. "You know, a temper tantrum, where you throw yourself on the floor and kick and scream."

I was silent for a moment, considering what to do. I had never in my life been in a situation remotely like this, and I didn't have a clue as to what my next move ought to be. A panic-stricken voice in my head was shrieking *Hidehidehide!* But where? While I lay sleeping and unaware, the enemy had broken through my defenses, breached my walls, penetrated to the secret center of my citadel. He was *in* my hiding place. So now what?

"Could you stop shining that light in my eyes?" I said finally.

"Oh. Sorry." The light swung away from me and then vanished with the flick of a switch.

The pupils of my eyes slowly began to readjust, and I could see a little better. He (for it was definitely a male who had invaded my world) loomed enormous in the narrow space. He must have simply put his head down and bulled his way through the passage. I wondered uneasily if he would be able to retreat or whether he was now a permanent fixture in my front hall.

A thought struck me.

"Are you . . . are you F?" I asked.

"Sure. How else would I know about A?"

"A?" I said, trying to keep my voice steady. "Who is A? Do you mean Andrea? I believe there is a girl of that name who lives here in the house. On the other side of the wall, of course. Very pretty," I added, vainly hoping that he would be tempted to go find her and leave me alone.

"No, not Andrea," he said scornfully. "I've known A wasn't Andrea for ages. And stop being so dumb, A. If you're not A, then how do you know about F?"

I was silent, stumped. He had me there, I had to admit.

He was silent too, except for some scuffling, creaking sounds as he tried to settle into a slightly more comfortable position. When he spoke again, his voice sounded a little less confident, almost defensive.

"I suppose you've been sitting here in your lair, laughing your head off about those letters?"

Surprised, I said, "Laughing? I'm sorry, did you mean them to be funny?"

To my amazement, he was immediately furious. "Is that supposed to be a joke or something?" he demanded, his face swelling ominously.

At this attack, every ounce of courage deserted me. "No! I'm s-sorry. Please don't be angry with me." A tear trickled down my cheek, and I quickly wiped it away.

"Hey," he said uncomfortably, "don't cry. C'mon, cut it out. I'm not mad at you. I didn't mean . . ." His voice trailed off. "This is so weird," he said at last. "This has got to be the strangest conversation —" He broke off and looked around himself and then back at me. "Does A stand for Anna? Is your name Anna?"

I simply stared at him, stricken, my tongue frozen in my throat.

"It is, isn't it? This is absolutely the most incredible thing I've ever heard. Kirsty wasn't lying? You're the youngest Newland daughter?"

"I am not!" I cried out, stung. "I'm almost two whole years older than Kirsty! And remarkably mature for my age."

F gaped at me. Then he burst out laughing. He threw his head back and roared with laughter. I clapped my hands to my ears, shocked at the dreadful clamor. Laughter like that did not belong here inside the wall.

"Oh, you are, are you? I can certainly tell." He ho-hohoed some more and then sobered. "Well, what are you *doing* here, crawling around inside the walls like a cockroach?"

"There are no cockroaches here!" I retorted hotly. "None! No mice or rats or termites or carpenter ants! I am *very* fussy about vermin."

"Well, *excuse* me," he said, grinning. He had a wide mouth in a round, plump face. He looked slightly familiar. "So you're kind of like the caretaker of this place, huh? And you make things for people, Kirsty said."

"Kirsty *told*," I murmured to myself, struck by this disloyalty for the first time.

"She didn't have much choice," F said. "I twisted her arm."

"You — you hurt my sister?" I said, terror and love warring in my breast.

"I didn't really," he said, sounding embarrassed. "I just said I would if she didn't tell me."

"You're nothing but a bully," I said stoutly, astounded at my own daring. I could feel adrenaline being released by the bucket load into my blood stream. Even a worm will turn, I discovered, if you come badgering and blustering into the very heart of its home.

"Aw, come off it. I didn't touch her, I only yelled some. It's just — I was sure she was the one. I thought Kirsty was writing those letters and then laughing at me. But she didn't seem like she knew what I was talking about, so finally I showed one to her and she guessed it was you."

I looked at him warily. Perhaps it was true that he hadn't actually raised a hand to Kirsty. Aware that I was venturing onto unknown terrain, I observed cautiously, "It seems to worry you that people will find your letters amusing."

"Not funny on purpose, dummy. Funny-stupid.

Like, how could a guy like me have any feelings at all about a girl like Andrea?"

"Why shouldn't you?" I asked carefully, afraid he would be angry again. "I don't see anything wrong with you." And I didn't. Now that I could see him properly, I realized that he was the young man who played the piano in the front parlor. In spite of his rather volatile temperament, I thought there was something sweet about his smile.

"Then you must be blind!" he exploded. "Everything's wrong with me! I'm fat, I'm clumsy, I'm stupid! I'm not even her age. I'm only fourteen."

As I had feared, he was angry again. However, having survived several blasts of ill-temper, I began to feel a bit more confident. I cringed, but only momentarily. I found that I was too interested in finding out what he would say next to stay frightened for long.

"I'm sorry," I said. "I didn't know."

He laughed, his bitterness vanishing in a moment. "Oh, stop being so humble. I like you better when you're being bossy and calling me a bully."

"Me, bossy?" I said, shocked to the core. "I'm *never* bossy."

"Oh, of course not, Ma'am," he said, smirking and clutching at himself in pretended fear. "I wouldn't dream of contradicting you, Ma'am!"

"You — are you *teasing* me?" I asked uncertainly.

"Well, sure I'm teasing you. Can't you tell? You

don't exactly accumulate a lot of social sophistication stuck here inside the boot closet, do you? And what are you up to back here, anyway? You never told me. Why doesn't anybody ever see you or talk about you? Hey," he said, shooting an apprehensive look at me, "there's not anything peculiar wrong with you, is there? I mean, you're not like the crazy wife in *Jane Eyre*? They kept her shut up because she liked to set fire to people in their beds."

"Of course not," I said with dignity. I had read *Jane Eyre* too. We had it in the library and it was a particular favorite of mine. "I'm perfectly normal in every way. Except that —"

"Except —?" he prompted, obviously poised for a hasty retreat, or at least as hasty a retreat as the width of my passageway and his bulk would allow. It almost made me laugh to see the expression on his face. He seemed actually frightened. Of me!

"Well," I said hesitantly, feeling the blood rush to my cheeks. "It's — I'm shy," I confessed.

He sat staring at me for several seconds and then he laughed. He laughed harder than he had when I'd told him that I was remarkably mature for my age. He held his stomach and gasped for breath. The walls creaked alarmingly as he rocked back and forth with laughter. "Ow! Ow, stop it, you're killing me!"

I looked at him helplessly. "I'm not doing anything," I said.

"You're shy. I'll say you're shy! You're an Olympic class wallflower, that's for sure!" And he burst out into roars of laughter again.

"Shhh!" I whispered. "Someone will hear you."

"Well, so what?" he said, and then, as he saw the expression on my face, "Sorry. I guess that would kind of spoil things for you, wouldn't it?"

When he had composed himself again, he said, "Wow. Shy isn't the word for you. How long have you been shut up in this little room?"

"Seven years. And it isn't only this little room, you know," I said, anxious to have my achievement admired. "It goes on forever, practically. I can go anywhere in the house I want. There are passageways and rooms all through the house."

But it was the first part of my response that seemed to impress him. *"Seven years?"*

"Almost seven and a half," I said, rather proud that he seemed to think it so remarkable.

"Seven and a half *years?"*

"Well, of course, I do come out at night sometimes when everyone's asleep."

"Oh, you do, do you?" He sounded a bit dazed. "Sorry. This is a little hard to accept. I mean, I knew something weird must be going on when Kirsty said that there was another Newland daughter no one had ever seen. Especially since —" he gestured at the house, "this place isn't exactly cut off from all outside human contact." As he spoke, what sounded like a drove of cattle came thundering down the stairs over our heads. He winced.

"I guess I just didn't believe it before. I figured Kirsty was spinning me tales to get rid of me, maybe to see how gullible I am. I *am* gullible, too," he said gloomily. "I have too much imagination. I'll believe anything. Especially if somebody like Kirsty says it. I always kind of liked her, even if she is a brat."

"Did she criticize you for being a carnivore?" I asked, worried.

"You bet she did. You'd think I was slaughtering a pig on the best furniture, the way she yelled. It was just a cold slice of pepperoni pizza left over from my lunch at school. To hear Kirsty tell it, the vast herds of pepperoni that once roamed our great land have all fallen to the butcher's knife because of people like me."

This, I decided, was a joke. I was almost certain there was no pepperoni animal. "Oh, Kirsty," I said, shaking my head. Nevertheless, I reflected, it didn't seem to have chased him away permanently.

"How did you know I wasn't Andrea? I was sure I had you fooled," I said wistfully.

"I saw one of my letters disappear inside the wall, for one thing. And then there was this big hullabaloo" (here I blushed) "coming apparently from inside the hall closet, only nobody was in there, and it had a false back. So I did some investigating — nobody notices what you do or where you go in this house. It took a couple of hours" (so I had slept for quite some time, it appeared) "before I found your entrance down in the basement." He looked smug at his own cleverness.

"And anyway," he went on, "are you kidding? I had some serious doubts right from your first letter. Andrea? Needlepoint?"

"I see what you mean," I said thoughtfully.

"I doubt Andrea can even thread a needle, let alone do French knots," he said cheerfully. He didn't sound as though he thought it was a serious flaw in her education.

I sighed.

"And the style never sounded like Andrea. She's more —" he glanced at me and hesitated.

"Sophisticated?" I suggested sadly.

"Well, yeah, kind of. What do you expect," he said, inexplicably angry again, "if you go and shut yourself up like this?"

"I don't know, F," I said meekly.

His frown softened and he laughed. "It's funny to hear you call me that," he said, smiling in a friendly way. "I don't mean to say that you're not a pretty original personality yourself. But of course I never thought you were *Andrea.*"

"No, of course not."

"Well, don't be so quick to agree with me," he said, annoyed all over again. I gave it up. There seemed to be no pleasing him.

"Anyway," he said, looking away from me and

blushing furiously. "You've read my letters. So I guess you know how I am about her. What's it like," he asked, "being her sister?"

I thought this over. It seemed a difficult question to answer offhand.

"I don't know. You probably know her better than I do. I haven't spoken to her in years. But you — you're one of her friends."

"Who, me? I most certainly am not."

"But then — you mean you're Kirsty's friend?"

"No. Don't you know what I'm doing in your house?"

I shook my head.

"My father's name is Frank Albright, and if I know anything about anything, you and I are about to become brother and sister, A."

I stared at him open-mouthed.

"Which means," he went on, "that I'm about to become Andrea's brother too. And if you think my chances with Andrea are hopeless now, picture the setup after our parents get married. Ask your stepsister out for a date and the cops'll throw you in the slammer for a thousand years. Seriously," he said dejectedly, "it's probably a felony or something."

This fate, I realized, would befall F no matter which of us he honored with his attentions. "Oh, dear," I said.

"No kidding," he agreed.

"But wait a minute," I said. "If you're F, and you're Frank Albright's son, then he can't marry my mother and we can't become brother and sister. He's —"

Just then we both heard it, a scuffling, bumping sound. The sound of yet another intruder climbing up from the basement, in through my front entrance.

All the world, it seemed, had chosen this afternoon to drop in on me unannounced and uninvited.

twelve

"Ow, ow! Oof!" this person said. "Oh, this is impossible!"

It was Kirsty. I couldn't see her at first because F was blocking the way into the room.

"Move, Francis," said her voice. "Is she here? Is Anna in here? Anna, are you dead?"

Francis! So that was F's real name.

"I can't move," he objected. "I'm wedged in here like a sardine."

"There's a lot more room further in," I said. "Your name is *Francis?*"

"Hey, there *is* more room further in. Why didn't you tell me before? I've been dying. Well, yes," he admitted, "my name is Francis. I'm Francis Chester Albright the Fourth. My dad is Francis Chester Albright the Third. And if he had a spark of decency, he'd let me call myself Frank too, but no, he says it confuses people."

"I think F is better," I said.

"Almost anything would be," he said sadly.

"Anna!" said Kirsty. She had now managed to squirm inside my secret room and crouched on the floor, staring at me. "Anna, you're alive! And you're so — so huge!"

F (for so I intend to continue calling him) gave a bark of laughter. I looked at him warningly and he whispered, "Sorry! But jeeze, Kirsty! You finally find your long-lost sister, and the first thing you do is ask her if she's dead. Then you turn around and accuse her of turning into a porker. And anyway, she isn't huge at all. She's tiny."

Kirsty shook her head. "You wouldn't think so if you knew what she used to look like," she said. She looked me over some more. "And you've changed, other ways, too."

"I've grown up," I said proudly. "So have you, Kirsty."

"Yes," she agreed, "but it's not just that. I can *see* you now."

"You can?" I said, not sure whether to be pleased or sorry.

"Well, sure she can," F said. "Did you think you were invisible or something?"

"Um," I said, and looked at Kirsty. She shrugged helplessly. "Not exactly," I mumbled.

"So this is where you've been all these years, Anna?"

Kirsty said, looking around. "In this tiny, tiny room? How can you stand it?"

"Oh, there's much more than this," I said.

"Where are we, anyway?" she asked, puzzled.

"I know," F said. "I figured it out. We're in the coat closet under the stairs."

"Don't be stupid, Francis," Kirsty said. "Look around you. Where are the coats? And don't you think that in seven years we'd have noticed Anna lurking in the coat closet?"

"The coats are over here, I think," F said, crawling over to the big end of the room. "Behind a partition. See? I can almost stand up."

"I'm telling you, Francis, you can see all the way to the back of the coat closet and it's *empty.*"

While they argued, it suddenly occurred to me that for the first time in my life I was playing hostess in my own home.

"Oh!" I cried, jumping as though I'd been bitten.

They both turned to stare at me.

"What's the matter, Anna?" Kirsty asked.

"I'm so sorry!" I said. "I haven't offered you anything to eat or drink."

Kirsty laughed and said, "Oh, Anna, it's so good to see you again," which seemed like an odd thing to say in response to my remark.

"Sounds like a good idea to me," F said. "Unless, of course, you normally eat sawdust and cobwebs or something. I'm pretty broad-minded about food, but there are limits. And don't offer Kirsty any roast mouse," he said with a wicked grin, "or she'll take a hatchet to you."

"I would n —" Kirsty began.

"I *told* you, there are no mice here," I said, annoyed.

Kirsty turned and stared at me. "Anna," she said in a wondering tone, "do you know what you just did?"

I shrank back a little. She went on staring at me, eyes wide with astonishment. My hands flew instinctively to my hair and face. Was my head dusty? Or was there a giant pimple blooming on my nose? If so, was that what F kept laughing about?

"N-no," I said nervously.

"You *interrupted* me. I was talking, but you wanted to say something, so you rode right over me."

I blushed deeply. Tears began to well up in my eyes. Seeing Kirsty for the first time in three years, and meeting F for the first time ever, I did so want everything to go well. And now I'd been rude and offended Kirsty. F would be completely disgusted with me.

"I'm sorry," I whispered.

"No, no!" Kirsty shook her head so vigorously that her hair flew around her face. "That's great, Anna, really!"

"It is?"

"Sure," F said. "If you didn't interrupt Kirsty now and then you'd never get a word in edgewise. Good

Lord, A, between Kirsty and Andrea, no wonder you retreated into the woodwork. The two of them never shut up."

Kirsty looked stricken. "Oh, do you think so? You mean Anna moved into the walls because of *us?*" She looked so like my tender-hearted little sister as she spoke that I reached out a hand toward her, but did not quite possess the courage to touch her knee.

"No, Kirsty," I said. "It's me, not you. It's the way I am, and there's nothing to be done about it. You know that."

"I do not know that," she responded with some spirit. "You've already done something about it. You've changed, Anna, you really have. I'm so relieved. I've been horribly worried, but now I think things may be okay after all."

"What do you mean," I asked apprehensively, "'Things *may* be okay after all'?"

"How about some of that food we were promised?" F interrupted. "I'm starving."

"Oh, of course," I said, blushing. "I'm so sorry. If you'll follow me —"

I was longing to show off my kingdom. If only they could see everything I'd done, they'd be so impressed. At least, I hoped they would be impressed. How wonderful it would be to have F admire me!

But F was clearly too large to move through my passages. He couldn't even begin to negotiate the section underneath the window seat in the dining room.

"I suppose you'd better stay here, F," I said regretfully. "Maybe Kirsty —?" Kirsty was definitely smaller than F, but I doubted that even Kirsty would be able to manage. My front hall was by far the largest passageway, and both F and Kirsty had had a struggle getting through.

With a jolt of cold fear, I realized that I was not so *very* much smaller than Kirsty these days. If I continued to grow . . .

"Anna, if you're expecting me to crawl through any more laundry chutes, you can just forget it. Sorry, but I think I'm developing an acute case of hydrophobia."

"You are?" I said, puzzled.

F clapped a hand over his mouth to suppress a snort of laughter. "Watch it, A! Your sister's got rabies. *Claus*trophobia, you idiot, claustrophobia!"

"Whatever," Kirsty said indifferently. "Anyway, I can't wiggle through slits in the walls. You may not have noticed, but," she leaned over to whisper in my ear, "I'm getting a figure."

I laughed nervously. "So am I," I whispered back.

"Oh, don't start in with that female stuff," F groaned. "Whispering and giggling and falling all over each other."

I looked at Kirsty and she giggled. I giggled too, experimentally. It felt nice, like soda fizzing inside of you. *Female stuff,* I thought happily. Kirsty and I were being women together, doing female stuff.

Kirsty beamed at me. "Anna," she said, "I can't believe you're actually here. D'you know, after I told Francis about you, I suddenly got this horrible feeling that you were just a story I'd made up as a little kid. I felt so dumb, like I'd admitted to believing in the Tooth Fairy or something."

This gave me rather a chill. That was exactly what I was afraid might have happened, that my family had ceased believing in my existence.

"Ladies," F said plaintively, "wasn't something said about food, like an hour ago? I'm a growing boy."

"Of course," I said quickly. "I'll go see what I can find. Um, excuse me, F, but I have to open that trap door that's right underneath you."

"Oh! Sorry." There was an awkward moment as they both tried to squeeze themselves into the small end of the room.

"How'd you get this damn chair in here, anyway?" F grumbled.

"Francis, ow!" Kirsty cried, "You've got your elbow in my eye!"

Finally they crawled out into the passage, where they could at least stand up, and waited as I opened the trap door.

"Where's that go?" F asked curiously, trying to peer down the hole from his position in the doorway to my secret room.

"No fair, I can't see anything!" came Kirsty's plaintive voice from without. We were being awfully noisy, I thought anxiously.

"It looks like a humongous heating duct," F said suspiciously.

"It *is* a heating duct," I said proudly. "But it isn't really hooked up to the furnace. It just looks like it. It goes under the side hall through the basement and comes up in the dining room. Then I have a passageway in the dining room through the window seat and the china closets on either side of the window. You have to crawl a bit, of course," I said brightly, trying to ignore the looks of incredulity on their faces, "but I don't mind a bit!"

"Oh, good," Kirsty said blankly.

"How do you carry the food?" asked F, whose mind certainly did seem to run on those lines.

"On a little cart," I answered. "I hold it with my teeth."

"Your teeth! How — how interesting." Neither of them seemed to know what to say after that, so I waved a jaunty farewell and tried to vanish gracefully down the hole. This was much more difficult than you might think, since it was necessary to go head first, to be sure of seeing where you were going. So naturally, the last they saw of me was my — well, you know.

In the kitchen I poured milk into three cups and cut up some brownies. When I returned with this little snack, Kirsty and F were quarrelling fiercely, apparently about me.

"You don't know anything about Anna," Kirsty said

angrily, as I crawled out of the heating duct. "So why don't you just butt out, Francis?"

"Well, if she's going to be my sister too —" F broke off when I handed him a brownie. "Oh, sorry, A, I didn't see you there. Kirsty," he commanded, shifting slightly so that he faced me, "tell her."

I looked at the two of them and my heart turned over.

"Kirsty? What is it?" I whispered.

Kirsty looked wretched. "Oh, Anna," she said, and the kindly childish tears welled up in her eyes. "Mom came to my room half an hour ago and asked me if I would mind having Mr. Albright for a stepfather and moving to Chicago."

Chicago!

"And when I said, 'What about Anna,' Mom got absolutely furious with me and said not to be so silly, and then Andrea came in and told me to grow up, for crying out loud, and then they both left the room talking about apartments on Lakeshore Drive. His father is stinking rich," she said, jerking her chin accusingly at F.

I reeled in shock and dismay. Or rather, I started to reel and then remembered in time that impulsive movements had their price. My whole body ached from my latest displays of emotion, and I had no desire to repeat the experience.

"Now, listen, A, I've been thinking. This shyness

thing," F said through a mouthful of brownie, "I'll bet we can beat it."

"Don't be stupid, Francis," Kirsty objected. "You can't expect Anna to go from *this*" she gestured at my secret room, "to a condominium overlooking Lake Michigan in a few weeks. No, be quiet Francis, and listen. All she has to do is let Mom and Andrea know that she's still alive and that she really exists. Then we can all stay here in Bitter Creek, which would be the best thing for everybody."

"What you mean is that *you* don't want to go to Chicago," F said.

"Nobody does, except for your father," Kirsty retorted. "And Andrea," she added fair-mindedly. "But she doesn't count because she's going away to college next year."

"Well, my father does want to go, and if he can't go he'll expect a good reason why not."

"Anna *is* a good reason," Kirsty said uneasily.

"Oh, unhuh, sure. What do you think his reaction would be if your mother said, 'Oh, yes, Frank. I forgot to mention that I have another daughter who lives inside the walls of this house and never comes out, so to avoid upsetting her you'll have to forget about Chicago, turn down the partnership deal, and we'll stay here in Bitter Creek for the rest of our lives'?"

Kirsty looked worried.

"I mean, my dad is a pretty nice guy, but be reasonable, Kirsty. If they're getting married, he's going to be Anna's stepfather. Bare minimum, he's going to insist on meeting her."

I winced.

"And when he does meet her, do you actually think he'll be willing to just let things go on the way they have?"

The answer to this was so obviously no that neither of us spoke for a moment. "She could always hide from him," Kirsty said at last in a tentative voice.

This sounded like an excellent idea. I looked hopefully at F.

F shook his head solemnly. "That won't work with my dad. I've heard him say lots of times that there's something fishy about the way this house is laid out. He'll figure it out, and then he'll find her." He turned to me. "A, listen to me. That could be bad, having my father come after you and dig you out of the walls. It would be much better if you didn't try to hide from him. He's awful stubborn."

I nodded a little, to show I understood. I could not move or speak for terror.

"Anyway," Kirsty said, "I don't think it's going to be so easy for you to hide anymore, Anna. You're just so much more — obvious — than you used to be." Kirsty turned to F. "So what are we going to do?"

F didn't answer immediately; he just looked at me. So she turned and looked at me too. The pressure of their two gazes gave me back the power of movement. I stealthily shifted position, trying to escape. To my dismay, their eyes followed me. So it was true; they could see me perfectly well.

"I'm afraid there's no other way," F said. "You're going to have to come out of the wall, A."

thirteen

"A party," F said. "A Halloween party."

"A *party*," Kirsty said scornfully. "That is the dumbest thing I ever heard in my life. Shy people absolutely hate parties."

It was two days later, and Kirsty and F were still squabbling over the details of my introduction into society. My terror slowly died down as I realized that nothing was going to happen to me immediately; that at least for the moment my only role was to listen to the debate raging around me and serve juice and cookies.

In any case, I had another card up my sleeve. I knew something, something that would completely derail any plans that Mother and Mr. Albright might have. It seemed a little odd, actually, that no one but I had noticed that a very definite impediment to the marriage existed. However, I felt reasonably secure, and in the meantime I was enjoying the novel experience of being fussed over by F and Kirsty.

"Listen," F said, "I've been doing some research on this . . ."

Kirsty groaned. F had gone to the public library and checked out a big stack of books about shyness (amazing! I never knew that such a body of literature existed) and now spoke a language largely incomprehensible to us, using terms like "agoraphobia" and "fear hierarchies," and debating the value of "flooding therapy" over "systematic desensitization."

I thought that this scholarship was very impressive and settled down contentedly with my sewing to listen and admire. Kirsty, on the other hand, seemed annoyed by F's cleverness. I suspect she rather resented the fact that she couldn't make heads or tails of what he was talking about.

"C'mon, Kirsty, listen. I mean it. We don't have time for all that gradual one-day-at-a-time stuff." F gestured vigorously with both arms as if he would create a brave new spirit for me out of thin air and his own will. His zeal received a bit of a check when he inadvertently banged his right hand on the underside of a stair tread. "Ow! That hurt." He broke off to suck his knuckles. "We'll just have to push her off the dock," he continued cheerfully, "and see if she can swim." His eyes brightened, and he actually rubbed his hands gleefully at the thought.

I gasped for air, feeling the metaphorical waters already closing over my head. I pictured a crowd standing on the shore, a sea of staring, critical faces watching me as I sank for the third time.

"And what if she can't swim?" Kirsty demanded.

I looked anxiously at F. I also wanted to know the answer to that question.

F looked impatient. "If she can't, she can't. We'll be right there," he said, turning kindly toward me. "Nobody's going to eat you, you know. It's just gonna be an uncomfortable hour or two."

I felt a little faint. An *hour* or two!

"There's nothing to worry about, A. I'll protect you."

F reached out and patted my arm.

I stared down at my arm, at the place where his hand had touched my skin, thinking to see a small charred spot where flesh had met flesh. My panic was gone, swallowed up in wonder. F had touched me, and I had not burst into flames or shattered like glass or sunk through the floor like a stone into a well. I rubbed the place on my skin gently. It didn't even hurt. How long, I wondered, had it been since anyone had touched me?

"Pay attention, A," F said. "This is the good part."

I sat up obediently and tried to give my mind to what he was saying. It was nice to know that there was going to be a good part.

"This," F continued triumphantly, "is where my plan is so brilliant. Don't you see? It'll be a Halloween party. A *costume* party."

"A costume party?" Kirsty asked, frowning.

"Sure," F said. "A costume party. Right up A's alley. She can go to the party and hide behind a mask! See?"

A costume party, I thought. Hmmmm . . .

"It might work," Kirsty admitted grudgingly. "And as a matter of fact, Andrea was talking last night about giving a Halloween party. How do you feel about it, Anna?"

"Would I have to talk to people?" I asked.

"No," said Kirsty.

"Yes," said F.

"Francis —" Kirsty protested.

"Kirsty," F said, "she has to start sometime. If we had more time, I'd say fine, let her get used to being around people first. But we *don't* have time. Once my dad gets the go-ahead for a project, he's like a runaway train. He'll drive straight through a brick wall to get where he's going."

I flinched.

"And, A," F continued persuasively, "if you can go to a party, a teen-aged party, and actually talk to people, maybe even dance with somebody, well, after that you can do anything, go anywhere. It's like a baptism of fire. You can never be as afraid again."

"How would you know?" Kirsty asked, smiling slyly at F. "I saw you at the Freshman Mixer last week. *You* didn't talk to anybody, and you sure didn't dance. When I said hi to you, you turned bright red and acted like you didn't hear me."

"What — what were you doing at the Freshman Mixer anyway?" demanded F, obviously a bit flustered. "You're a seventh grader. You're supposed to stick with the middle-school kids."

Kirsty haughtily explained that she had been invited by a ninth-grade girlfriend, but I wasn't listening.

"I *can't* dance," I said sadly.

"Oh, that's easy," F said. "Don't worry. We'll teach you. I do know how." He looked coldly at Kirsty. "I just didn't feel like it that night." He turned to me. "It's easy. You sort of wiggle around to the beat of the music."

"No, I mean I just couldn't. With — with a boy, you mean?"

"I don't see why it has to be a boy," Kirsty said. "Half the couples at dances are two girls anyway. I'll dance with you, Anna. You'll see, it'll be fun."

"*I'll* dance with you, A," F said, frowning. "You won't be afraid to dance with me, will you?"

"N-no," I said. I pictured F and me, waltzing all alone in an immense, shadowy ballroom. The music swelled to a crescendo and F swept me away, cradling me tenderly in his arms. We danced exquisitely together, our steps matching perfectly.

"I'll dance with you," I said, lowering my eyes and blushing a little.

"That is," Kirsty said acidly, "if boring old Andrea doesn't happen to look in his direction. Too bad if she does, Anna, because he'll completely forget about you.

He'll spend the rest of the night mooning around, hoping she'll do it again. Francis has a crush on Andrea," she informed me. "Along with the rest of the males in America," she concluded gloomily.

"I know," I said sadly.

F folded his arms and attempted to look dignified.

"Which is *so* stupid," Kirsty said spitefully. "Andrea's fallen in love at long last, and not with Francis, that's for sure."

F turned away, and would not look at us.

"With Foster Addams," she explained, apparently determined to crush any hopes he might still cherish. "That's why she's so hot to move to Chicago. Foster Addams's family is moving to Chicago at Christmas. His dad works for the same company your dad does."

F looked stricken, and my heart nearly broke for him. I groped in my mind for something to make it up to him, to make him smile. But what could *I* do that would compensate him for the loss of Andrea?

"I'll dance with anyone you like, F," I offered, my heart pounding uncomfortably in my throat. "I — I'll *ask* someone, a totally strange boy, to dance. I will," I repeated stubbornly, as they stared at me in amazement. "I'll be brave, you'll see. You'll be proud of me."

"Anna, no!" Kirsty said, horrified. "We wouldn't expect you to do anything like that! I wouldn't have the nerve for that myself. Not a total stranger, anyway."

"I'm not afraid," I said, although I was, very much.

"But, Anna —" Kirsty protested.

"Let her be," F said. "She's got guts." To me he said, "We're proud of you already. You'll be great, A."

"Yes," I agreed, "I will."

In my dark corner I straightened my spine, assuming the carriage and posture of a queen. I *was* a queen at that moment: clever, charming, and kind. And brave, heartbreakingly brave. My eyes swam with sudden tears at my own courage.

I wanted F to understand how splendid my offer was. He admired me now; he would admire me more when he realized that my pledge had been given for entirely unselfish, disinterested reasons. "But, of course," I confided, "you know that none of this is actually necessary."

"What do you mean, Anna?" asked Kirsty, curious.

"It is too necessary, A," said F, frowning. "No backing out, now. You promised."

"Certainly I promised," I said with dignity. "And what I have promised I will deliver, you can be quite sure about that. I only mean what I said. None of this is necessary. The marriage cannot take place."

"What?" "Huh?" They stared at me, wholly mystified. I didn't like it. *Why* hadn't anyone else thought of this? Mentally clutching the tattered edges of my imaginary queen's robe about me, I tried to carry it off with a high hand.

"How can you have forgotten, F?" I asked reproachfully. "Your mother. In one of your letters you referred to a mother in the present tense. Unless she has suddenly expired, your father is a married man. And even if she did just die, I call it indecent, marrying only weeks after a spouse's death." The looks on their faces almost made me despair. "But," I concluded in a rush, "I don't think she *has* died or you'd have said, and the law must have changed an awful lot since I last checked if it's legal for a man who's already married to marry our mother."

"Oh, Anna," said Kirsty sorrowfully.

"For cryin' out loud, A! They're divorced. Two years ago," F said. "Weekends I live with her, and weekdays I live with him."

"Oh," I said. "Oh."

My defenses crashed about me. There was nothing to stop the marriage after all. They would marry and move to Chicago, as sure as fate. And I —

"How long is it until Halloween?" I asked in a strangled voice.

"A whole two weeks," Kirsty said comfortingly.

In two weeks I would be out in the open under harsh lights, no doubt wearing an ill-judged costume that would make me look like a fool and a freak and a geek, standing before some conceited, boorish boy with sadistic tendencies. There I would be, baldly begging this vulgar lout to take me in his arms and caper about with me across the floor in full view of a crowd of total strangers. And this entertainment would last only *an hour or two.*

My thoughts went further; I waded deeper and

deeper into despair. Even if I survived this experience, there was all the future to dread. My mother would marry, yes, and what sort of a man would he be? A divorced man. A man leaving a trail of broken hearts behind him, a man who was obviously yearning for the opportunity to break some more. The fact that he would one day inevitably grow bored with my mother and toss her aside was cheering, but it wasn't as much of a comfort as you might expect. He wouldn't desert her until *after* we had left Bitter Creek and our beloved home.

And then of course, we would be homeless. We would be expelled from his luxurious penthouse on Lakeshore Drive, four waifs drifting aimlessly through the alleyways and sewers of Chicago, at the mercy of the wind and the rain and the snow and the evil leers of passersby.

We sat in silence for a bit. There didn't seem to be anything to say.

"I think . . ." F murmured thoughtfully. I waited. Surely darling, kind, wonderful F would now say something that would make things at least a little bit bearable.

"I think I'll come as a ghost," he said. "That's easy, and then Andrea won't know who I am. If I disguised my voice, we could probably have a really long conversation without her even guessing it's me."

I sighed.

fourteen

"Cleopatra, Queen of the Nile," I mused. Slowly I drew thick black barbaric lines around my eyes. I backed away from the mirror to study the effect. I had painted cloth and wood before, but never skin. It was interesting, really; a whole new medium for conceal-ment. The liquid eyeliner felt heavy and strange, weighting down my eyelids, making them look sensu-ous and cruel.

I reddened my lips and wrapped a black cloth around my mouse-colored hair. Then I arranged my-self in a classic two-dimensional Egyptian pose before the mirror.

"Hmmm . . ." I said. In my fringed tunic I looked like a giant moth with cruel and sensuous eyes.

"The clothes are wrong," Kirsty said, pushing for-ward to take her turn at the mirror. She had draped herself in yards and yards of faded purple velvet. "Take them off," she ordered.

I blushed, and clutched defensively at my tunic.

"Not all of them, you idiot," Kirsty said. "Just down to your underwear. Then we can kind of wrap you up in this white sheet. Oh, here! Take the sheet and go try it on behind that screen, if you're so modest. You're as bad as my friend Shana. She always hides in the bathroom to get dressed for dance class instead of doing it with the rest of us."

Thoughtfully, I retired behind the screen in the corner of the south attic. Kirsty and I had come up to my sewing workroom to rummage through fabrics and try to decide on costumes. Instead of squeezing through my passageways, she had simply walked up the attic stairs, where I unlocked the door and admitted her.

"Wow!" she'd exclaimed, staring at the hundreds of bolts of material, skeins of yarn, racks of trim and thread, cutting tables and scrap bins. "I had no idea! Though I suppose I should have guessed. When I was little I thought you just waved your magic wand and poof! There was a new dress or whatever." She fingered a length of figured silk. "Why didn't we ever come up here looking for you? Why didn't we ever even think of it?" Her eyes were forlorn.

"The door was locked," I explained gently.

She looked obstinate. "We should have knocked it down."

Now I asked casually from behind the screen, "Why won't Shana get dressed with the rest of you? Is she — is she malformed, or something?"

Kirsty sputtered. "Malformed? No, of course not. I don't know, we're all like that, sort of. The other day Maybeth William's older brother and two of his friends came by to pick her up after dance class. They got there early and stood there in the doorway staring at us in our leotards and tights. Lisa Applebaum screamed and pointed at them, and everybody *ran* for the changing room. Me too," she admitted. "And it's dumb, because a year ago I would have been showing off like crazy for them. I love to dance. Maybe I'll be a ballerina for Halloween," she reflected, and executed several pirouettes before the mirror. "Only," she gasped, staggering a little and hanging onto the mirror for support, "I've been a ballerina for Halloween like about six times already."

I emerged from behind the screen gripping the sheet insecurely about me and approached the mirror dubiously.

"'Lo, the beautiful one comes,'" Kirsty said kindly.

"I can't go to a party like *this*," I said, grabbing frantically at various parts of my body.

"Well, no," Kirsty said. "I figured you'd make it into one of those skimpy little nightgown things Egyptians wore."

"I can't wear a skimpy little nightgown to my first party, Kirsty," I said, feeling the panic rise in my throat.

"Okay, okay," she said pacifically. "Let's think of

something else." She looked at me sharply. "Anyway, I'd think you'd feel more comfortable with a bra on."

"Oh!" I said, blushing hotly. "You mean —"

"I mean you're getting pretty well developed. They stick out, you know, especially if you get chilled, like you are now."

I clutched miserably at my chest. I had noticed that, too. "I never knew what a bra was for," I confessed humbly.

"Oh, you have to wear one," Kirsty said authoritatively. "Or else when you get older they go all droopy and fall off or something."

I stared down aghast at my newly acquired bosom. "I'll start making some right away," I said faintly.

"I'll go get you one of mine," Kirsty offered, "and you can wear it until you've made yours."

Half an hour later, feeling very grown-up, but also rather as though I was wearing a dog harness, I sat thumbing through a book called *Lives of Famous Women*, looking for a costume idea.

Kirsty had earlier given me an explanation of my periodic bleeding. She told me about babies and how they come, and provided me with a bag of disposable pads that were to be worn in my underclothing for those days every month. I later found the pad to be useful, even though it gave me the odd sensation of riding a very small horse.

I must tell you, frankly, that the explanation she

offered sounded far-fetched, to say the least, and I couldn't help but wonder if she hadn't got it wrong somehow. The part about men and women and what they do to each other in bed I don't even mention; it's too grotesque to be taken seriously.

But that the bleeding was a fact I knew from my own experience. And even though it was a great comfort to think that I wasn't the only one so afflicted, it was hard to believe that every woman in the world had to deal with this monthly embarrassment for the majority of her adult life. The only escape, according to Kirsty, was either old age or pregnancy.

Flipping through the pages of *Lives of Famous Women*, I tried to imagine Jackie Kennedy and Marie Antoinette suffering from such a messy disability sixty days out of the year. Did Queen Elizabeth have a "period"? How about Madame Curie? Strange to think that while these women ruled empires and studied the properties of radioactivity, their bodies were patiently, single-mindedly preparing for pregnancy and childbirth over and over again, despite all previous disappointments.

I looked down at my own body with awe and not a little unease. Perhaps my body didn't want the same things I did; it apparently had plans and schemes I knew nothing about. Perhaps one day it would betray me in some unexpected way. But how could that be? We were one and the same being.

"Hey!" Kirsty interrupted my musings. "Would you make me a cat costume? All slinky and sexy. I love cats and Mom won't let me have one."

I looked at her consideringly. "Y-es," I said. "Black velvet would make a nice cat suit. We'd have to think how to manage your tail so you don't drag it. With a red feather boa around your neck and a golden crown, you could be the Queen of Cats," I suggested.

Kirsty's eyes lit up. "I love it!" she said. "Oh, would you please, Anna? I want to be the Queen of Cats!"

Suddenly I wished I had chosen that idea for myself. An animal costume would call for a mask that covered my whole head. Very well, I would forget about being a famous woman. Just for the moment I didn't want to be a woman anymore. I would unsex myself and be a squirrel, say, or a turtle. No doubt these animals came in male and female varieties, but at least they had the decency not to advertise their differences.

"A moth!" I said aloud. "I'll be a moth." Seeing Kirsty's dubious face, I explained how I had always admired the moth's ability to camouflage itself against a variety of backgrounds.

Kirsty shook her head. "Not a moth, Anna. A butterfly, maybe, but not a moth."

"Well, all right, I suppose," I said, privately resolving to find the drabbest, dullest butterfly in the book.

And so it was decided. Kirsty was to be a cat and I was to be a butterfly. Instead of *Lives of Famous Women*, we pored over books about cats and insects. After looking at the color plates in Peterson's *Field Guide to the Insects*, Kirsty decided to let me be a moth after all.

"Oh, good," I said, relieved.

"But only if you let me pick which one."

I nodded happily. There were little white moths, I knew, and gray ones, and any number of brown ones. I hoped she would pick brown. The color seemed to suit me, somehow.

"A luna moth," she said triumphantly, turning the book so I could see.

I winced. The luna moth was a great gaudy thing with sweeping, extravagantly tailed wings and a regal featherlike headdress. It was colored a brilliant poison green.

"But —" I protested.

"You said I could pick," Kirsty said, and ruthlessly swept on, "Look, over there! That cloth right there's exactly the right shade for the wings."

I studied the illustration and then inspected the bolt of material she'd indicated. "No," I shook my head. "Not that one."

"Now, listen, Anna," Kirsty said bossily, sounding so much like herself as a small child that I had to smile, "don't you go trying to make this costume fade into the background. You're going to be a luna moth, and luna moths don't fade into the background."

"Don't worry, Kirsty," I said a little sadly. "I won't

make the luna moth costume fade into the background. As much as I might like to, I couldn't."

"Why not?" she asked suspiciously.

"Because . . ." I wrestled with the problem. It was hard to say why, exactly, but I really couldn't do it. "It would be wrong," I said helplessly. "It would be cheating. I have my self-respect as a craftswoman to think of. But that color green isn't right. And the texture is wrong."

I looked around myself discontentedly. There were still mountains of materials here, but I was beginning to run out of some things. It was annoying. "I don't think I have anything in that shade. I guess I'll have to hand-paint some silk to get just the right effect," I murmured. "I'd have had to do that anyway, even if I had the proper color. And maybe use some wire boning inside the wings . . ."

Satisfied, Kirsty left me rummaging about amongst my supplies and began painting whiskers on her upper lip with the liquid eyeliner.

Making the costumes kept me very busy for the two weeks before the party. There was no time for anything; no time even for terror, only a few odd snippets of panic sandwiched in between frenzied bouts of cutting and sewing. Kirsty wouldn't even let me see F. She didn't want him to know what our costumes would be. She said she wanted it to be a surprise. I wrote to him, though, and he wrote back, and I had to be content with that. His father, he said, had hinted at the marriage, but nothing further had developed on those lines. F thought that our mother was still stalling. *Oh, good, kind Mother!* I thought.

I measured every inch of Kirsty, a luxury I had not had for years. Always before I had had to measure by eye through a crack in the wall. Because her cat costume was to fit so closely, however, I needed to have exact measurements; I would be able to mold the cat skin onto her almost as neatly as her own.

Kirsty made an athletic and bouncy Queen of Cats. Noisy as it was, she could not resist pouncing and leaping all over the attic to try out her velvet paws and tiny sharp claws. Her tail was made of velvet-covered wood, cleverly segmented and jointed so that it was self-supporting and writhed with a life of its own.

Her mask-head was constructed of papier-mâché over a superstructure of wire. I made it as light as possible, but naturally she complained anyway. At least, she complained until she realized that she could, by pulling one of the whiskers, cause the jaw to drop and reveal the lower half of her smiling face behind two rows of gleaming pointed teeth. Two other whiskers controlled the eyelids so that she could blink or wink at will.

After that, she became a bit of a trial. She was a mass of twitches, winking and rolling her eyes, waving her tail, butting me skittishly with her crown, hissing and swatting at dust motes as they fell through the lingering beams of an autumnal sunset. Still, I could not help but laugh at her; she was enjoying her costume so much.

She turned stubborn again over my mask. I had planned to make a mask-head like hers, which would completely cover my whole head, but she refused to let me do it.

"It'll get hot and uncomfortable after a while, and you'll want to take it off," she protested. "And then where will you be, without makeup or anything to hide your face?"

I shook my head. I had long ago schooled myself not to mind discomfort. So long as my disguise remained intact, my hiding place undiscovered, I didn't much care about anything else.

"Well, it won't look right," she argued, shrewdly realizing that this was the better line of attack. "Look at the picture. The animal hardly even has a head; it's just a bump without a neck. No mouth even. You couldn't get the right look unless you cut your own head off. And that," she said hastily, seeing my speculative eyes, "is going way too far for the sake of accuracy.

"You'd be much better off wearing a circlet on your head with those feathery antennae things attached. And then we'll slick back your hair and paint your face kind of like you did for Cleopatra." When I still looked hesitant, she said, "And you could carry a little green sequined eye-mask with a stick on one side so you could cover your eyes when you felt shy. It'd look *good*, you know it would, Anna."

"Well-l . . ." She might actually be right, I decided. "I suppose I could," I said grudgingly.

fifteen

"Anna! Oh, Anna, you look wonderful," Kirsty whispered.

It was the night of the Halloween party.

I stared straight into the eyes of the young woman in the mirror. She was dressed in brilliant poison green, a clinging, slithery gown of painted silk, with dramatic floor-length sleeves. Her small, regal head was supported by a slender white neck, her hair sleeked back into a shining knot at the nape and crowned with a silver circlet adorned by two huge barbaric featherlike antennae.

"You'd never guess a moth costume could be so *glamorous.*"

Kirsty came and stood next to me in her cat suit. "Look," she said. "I think you've grown two inches in the last two weeks. We're the same height now. Anna, you really do look gorgeous. You're going to knock 'em dead, kid."

I continued staring at my reflection in the mirror.

"I think I'm going to throw up," I said finally.

"Oh, Anna, don't be so silly."

"No, I really think —"

"Anna, stop that right now. You're fabulous, a knockout, and you know it."

"I *know* I'm going to —"

"Eeeuuw! Here! Here, take this old pot thing. Not on your new dress, you idiot! Oh, Anna, how gross."

After an interval I said, "Thank you. I feel much better now. I'll just go dispose of this and rinse out my mouth and then I'll be quite ready."

"Really? I mean — are you sure you're okay?"

"No," I said steadily, wiping my mouth, "I am not sure I'm okay at all, but I promised F, and I promised you, that I would do this thing and I am going to do it."

"Well," Kirsty said dubiously, "if you say so . . ."

"I do say so."

"You promise you're not going to do that again?"

"I can't promise a thing," I said grimly. "Now, Kirsty, *please* —"

"Okay, okay," she said hurriedly. "Let's go."

Kirsty unlocked the attic door, and I stepped out onto the stair. The attic was my territory; the attic stair was not. I was now out of the wall and into the great world. Oddly, I felt no panic. I felt nothing. I was numb all over, except for a small cold spot in the pit of my stomach.

We walked down the stair to the second-story hallway. I paused a moment to look around me. I had been here often, of course, but only at night, in the dark, while everyone around me slept. It could not be said to be very brightly lit now. Kirsty had argued that a Halloween party should be a little shadowy and dark, and she had gone around replacing the sixty-watt bulbs with forties. Then she had festooned every wall, window, and doorway with artificial cobwebs. It occurred to me that some people might say she had gone a little overboard on the cobwebs.

"What do you think?" she asked eagerly. "There's lots more cobwebs downstairs. I used bags and *bags* of the stuff. It started to run out by the time I got up here. Isn't it spooky? And dark. I knew you'd like that."

I rummaged around in my mind for something to say. "It's probably exactly like the inside of a luna moth's cocoon," I said, pleased to have found a comment that was both flattering to her and comforting to me.

"You're right," she said, delighted. "I'll bet that's what it does look like. And you're about to emerge from the cocoon. It's perfect!"

That thought was less comforting, though true. I made a quick trip to the bathroom to freshen up and reapply some lipstick. Then we began to descend the great mahogany staircase. As we came around the bend, we paused on the landing to survey the crowded front hall.

"Most people are here already," Kirsty said. "I thought you'd rather wait till the place was full before you made an appearance. That way people won't wonder where you came from."

"Is — is F here?" I asked, beginning to feel my heart thumping softly under my ribs. I looked out over the throng, trying to find a familiar face. It was true that there were lots more cobwebs downstairs. It was difficult to make out any details of the room at all; everything was draped and masked in white spun plastic. It gave an odd and appropriately eerie effect. Costumed revelers seemed suspended in the strange, muffled light, like brightly colored fish swimming in nests of cotton wool.

"I don't — wait! There he is, that ghost over there in the flowered sheet. Wave to him. He's not gonna believe it when he sees you. Wave, Anna, wave. He doesn't see me."

Hesitantly I raised my hand waist-high and essayed a tiny flutter of the wrist.

"C'mon, Anna, get your arm *up* there. Oh, forget it. He's seen Andrea."

Both arms shot up into the air and I waved vigorously.

He saw me. So did everyone else in the room. I had

forgotten that we were standing alone on an elevation above a crowd, and that I was wearing a very striking costume. The tails of my shimmering green wings fluttered as I waved and I looked, no doubt, as though I was about to launch myself into the air and swoop down over them.

My worst nightmare had come true: eighty eyes at least were upon me. People pointed at me and said things; I could not hear what. I froze, motionless, still in my dramatic pose.

Kirsty realized the mistake and gave me a sharp push. I lowered my arms and abruptly began to descend the stairs, hanging on to the railing to keep from falling. A buzz of commentary rose to meet me as I dropped in altitude. My natural inclination was to stare at the floor to avoid the eyes of the multitude, but if I lowered my chin I was absolutely certain that my crown would slip forward. And, in my opinion, a tipsy moth with her crown falling off would look even more foolish than a haughty moth with her nose in the air, so I concentrated on gazing just above people's heads. This made it difficult to find F when I finally reached the bottom of the stair, but Kirsty grabbed me firmly by the arm and guided me.

"Is that you, A?" F gasped when I was steered up to him. "I don't believe it."

"Can we leave? Just for a moment," I begged, half fainting. I held my mask up before my face like a shield. "Into the kitchen or the butler's pantry. While I catch my breath."

"Great costume," someone said into my ear. "Incredible entrance. Do I know you? Are you in Drama Club or something?"

I turned. Kirsty and F were entirely blocked by this person, a medieval executioner, to judge by his attire. A black hood completely covered his head and he carried a plastic axe. The whole costume was mass-produced, I decided; the hood was made out of the cheapest cotton broadcloth, and I spotted obviously faulty seam construction in the vest. He was tall, taller than F, with large muscular arms and legs. I didn't see how I could escape if he wanted to talk to me.

Then it occurred to me that he fit the requirements for my grand gesture: he was a strange boy. I could accomplish my goal within minutes of arriving at the party. I took a deep breath.

"Do you want to dance?" I asked.

He seemed slightly taken aback, although it was hard to tell when all I could see of his face were his eyes through the slits in his black hood. What did I care? I had fulfilled my promise. It didn't matter if he said no. In fact, I very much hoped that he would say no. I wanted to dance with F, not with this tacky hired assassin. I only had to endure the moment of humiliation when he turned me down flat and the worst of my ordeal was over. I closed my eyes, waiting.

"Sure. How about a little later, seeing as how there's no music playing at the moment?"

True. I hadn't thought about it, but no one else seemed to be dancing. Perhaps that was why. I opened my eyes.

"Never mind," I said quickly. "That's okay." I looked over the executioner's shoulder for F. Had he heard? Did he know how courageous I was? Would this conversation never be over?

Apparently not.

"Hey, don't get all huffy. I'll dance without music, since you insist. Come on." He gripped me by the wrist and I was dragged, protesting feebly, away from the small circle of protection around Kirsty and F.

"Over here where there's more room." To my horror I realized that he meant to do what Kirsty called "slow dancing," which meant simply rocking back and forth in an intimate embrace. In public. His arm encircled my waist, and he placed my hand on his chest and held it there firmly with his own.

Then he began to sing.

Softly, I'm glad to say. Actually, he had quite a nice tenor voice, I must admit. I don't follow contemporary music, so I don't know the name of the song he sang, but I remember it was about love, which was rather alarming, to say the least. Slowly he began to move around the floor, his body swaying gently against mine. I shuffled along as gracefully as I could. I found that the combination of the high-heeled slippers that Kirsty had forced me to wear and my long sweeping wings made it necessary to lower my mask and use that hand to cling to him. Otherwise I was very much afraid that I would trip and fall at his feet.

He went on singing, looking deep into my eyes. I stared back like a bird hypnotized by a snake. Slowly I slipped into a sort of trance state, fitting the rhythmic movements of my body to his. This alien boy seemed to envelop me entirely, his arms, his scent, his voice, and yet, amazingly, I lived. It occurred to me that I would survive this. Perhaps when I was an old, old woman, I might even enjoy remembering it.

Finally his song drew to an end. We stopped, and I was conscious of a fleeting sensation of regret. Dancing wasn't so bad.

He released my hand but not my gaze and slowly pulled off his mask. He stood there smiling down at me, revealed as a classically handsome adult male. He had brown, crisply curling hair, a broad, mobile mouth, and brilliant violet eyes. His left arm was still around my waist, I realized.

"There," he said. "I danced with you. Now will you tell me who you are?"

My mind went blank. Who was I? Kirsty had come up with a name and life history I was supposed to produce if anyone asked me. To be honest, I really hadn't paid any attention since I'd planned on fainting if anyone actually spoke to me. In the event, unconsciousness seemed no more than a golden, unattainable dream.

"I —" I stammered. "I'm no one. I'm nobody," I clarified.

"So you're a mystery woman, is that what you're telling me? Come on," he said coaxingly, bending that overpowering masculine beauty over me. "Who are you? I'll swear I've never seen you before. Did you just move to Bitter Creek?"

"Let's dance some more," I suggested.

He smiled, a slow, lazy smile. "You're really something, you know it?"

I groped for some way to *force* him to dance again. In order to dance he had to sing and he couldn't sing and ask questions at the same time. "You have a wonderful voice," I offered, looking nervously up at him from under my lashes.

"Yeah? You think so?" This was obviously the right thing to say. "I want to be a singer in a rock band, but my parents are making me go to college. We've got this great group together — maybe you've heard of us? The Flying Pits? Anyway, we *would* be good if we had a decent drummer." He scowled at the thought of the drummer.

Well, at least he wasn't quizzing me about my name and antecedents. "What's wrong with the drummer?" I asked cunningly.

He opened his mouth to answer and then stopped, grinning at me.

"You're trying to get me to stop asking about your name, aren't you? Who *are* you? Come on, now I've *got* to know."

"You — I don't know who you are either." Actually, I thought I did. The voice, the name of the band, the classic good looks, all suggested the same name.

"If I tell you who I am, will you tell me who you are?"

At that moment, music began to play. In desperation I flung myself at him, like flinging a bone to a dog to stop his barking. I reached out and grabbed his hand and curled my body in to fit his.

"Dance with me," I pleaded, "this is my favorite song." Actually, I have no recollection of the song; it could have been a funeral march for all I knew or cared.

He laughed. "Okay, okay. Whatever this lady wants, she gets, apparently." He grasped my chin between finger and thumb and tilted my face up to his. "But I'll tell you something: I'm going to find out before the night is over. So," he said as we began to dance again, "you don't know who I am either, huh?" He was holding me closer this time. "Just to show you how generous I am, I'll tell you my name."

"That would be nice," I mumbled into his chest. My nose was mashed up against his pectoral muscles; I could barely breathe.

"My name is —"

"Foster Addams," a cold voice concluded for him. "Hello, Foster. Who's your friend?"

I writhed around in Foster Addams's arms, trying to get a view of the newcomer. I knew that voice.

Treading heavily on his foot, I persuaded him to loosen his grip. I peered out of his embrace like some wild animal peering out of the underbrush.

It was Andrea.

sixteen

"Hi, Andrea." Foster Addams released me and bestowed his sleepy smile on Andrea. "Don't you know who this is, either? Pretty cool outfit, huh? Look." He grabbed my hand, raised it over my head, and twirled me around for Andrea's inspection. Caught off guard, I fell back at the end of the twirl against Foster, with my other arm spread out against his chest for balance.

"Very impressive," Andrea said in the same icy tones.

He seemed unconcerned by her lack of enthusiasm. "You're pretty good on your feet," he said admiringly to me. "You ought to be a dancer. You vant to do de tango viz me?" He put his arm around me, shot our joined hands out shoulder-high and lurched sideways, dragging me with him.

"That was, without question, the worst Spanish accent I've ever heard," Andrea said.

"But you gotta admit, Babe, I can tango like the devil himself." Foster abandoned me and clutched

Andrea to his chest, staggering bent-kneed and stiff-armed into a corner with her and then back again. This maneuver seemed to improve Andrea's mood only marginally.

She was dressed as a mermaid. My eyes widened as I took in the shoddy handiwork. *Where* had Andrea picked up such trash? Surely she of all people ought to be able to recognize quality when she saw it. Suddenly I realized that she had noted and correctly interpreted my incredulous stare at her costume. This, I could not help but feel, was unfortunate.

"Who are you?" she asked bluntly. "This is my party and I have the right to know."

"I'm a friend of Kirsty's," I said. I looked around for Kirsty. With any luck, she would materialize and tell me who I was. There she was, half the room away, pulling her whiskers and making her eyes blink and her jaw open and close for an admiring group of people.

Andrea's gaze travelled over me. Uncomfortable, I held up the green jewelled mask to my eyes in a vain attempt to hide from her scrutiny.

"*Kirsty's* friend," she said, sounding not much friendlier. "Remarkably mature for your age, aren't you?"

"Yes, yes, I am," I said eagerly, pleased to be on familiar ground. I only hoped she wouldn't find this as laughable as F had. "Everyone has always said so, anyway," I amended.

I needn't have been afraid that she would laugh. An

almost murderous look passed over her features. I cowered backward, bumping into Foster.

"Hey, Andrea, geez," he said, placing a protective arm around me. "You're scaring the poor kid."

"The poor *kid* is right," Andrea retorted. "Doing a little cradle robbing, Foster? How old do you think she is?"

He turned and looked at me. "I dunno, sixteen, seventeen."

"*Twelve!* The *poor kid* is twelve years old."

Foster dropped his arm from my shoulder.

"I am not!" I said indignantly. "I was fourteen last August nineteenth."

"Oh, well." Foster seemed unsure that fourteen was a big improvement on twelve.

"August nineteenth?" Andrea looked startled. I thought I knew why, but I had to ask.

"Why are you surprised?" I asked.

"Because — because I don't see why somebody like you should be friends with Kirsty," she answered, looking mulish.

"Kirsty has other friends my age," I said confidently. Hadn't Kirsty said a ninth-grade girlfriend once invited her to a dance? "But that's not what surprised you," I pursued, with freshening courage. "You were surprised by the day I was born."

Andrea shrugged dismissively. "I used to know somebody with that birthday, that's all."

I smiled. She didn't say she was surprised because it

was the same as her own birthday, which would be reasonable. No, she said that she used to know somebody *else* with that birthday.

Foster frowned. "Weren't you born in August?" he asked.

"Y-es," Andrea admitted reluctantly. "That day. The nineteenth."

"Do I look like her?" I asked boldly, removing the mask from my eyes.

Andrea became very still. Then she turned her head and stared at me for a long, time-without-end moment. Her eyes searched mine. She examined my face, my hair, my waving antennae, my dress. Her eyes swept back up to mine.

"Excuse me," she said and, gathering up her mermaid's tail, she fled out of the room.

"Wuh-ho!" exclaimed Foster. His handsome face went stupid with amazement. He looked at me. "Huh?" he inquired. He seemed to be groping for the power of human speech and failing.

Unable to explain, I fell back on my usual conversational ploy with Foster Addams. "Shall we dance?" I suggested, with an insouciant little wave of the hand.

At that moment, Kirsty and F appeared. *Finally.* Kirsty had removed her head-mask and F his faded flowered sheet in order to gape at Foster and me.

Foster Addams did not seem to see them, although

they were standing at his elbow. "Are you really only fourteen?" he asked, wrapping his arms around me again and beginning to dance.

I nodded.

He drew back far enough to study my face. "I guess that's not *that* young," he said doubtfully. My age, however, did seem to put a damper on his enthusiasm. His grip was relatively loose and he didn't talk much. When the dance was over, he took my chin in hand again and smiled down at me.

"Listen, mystery woman," he said, "gimme a call in a couple of years. You're gonna be a little heartbreaker, you know it? And a woman to be reckoned with, I might add. Any fourteen-year-old who can dispose of Cast-Iron Andrea in three minutes flat is a power in the land. Hell," he said, his grin widening, "you're a little heartbreaker right now. Here —" He looked around us and, seeing F standing there goggling at us, he grabbed him by the arm. "This guy looks like he's about fourteen. Go break *his* heart." To F he said, "Watch out for this one. She's a dancing fool." He leaned over and kissed my forehead. "Toodles, kid," he said, and off he went, waving a lordly farewell with his plastic headsman's axe.

"Thank you, Foster," I said serenely. "Goodbye." I turned to F and produced my foolproof line: "Would you like to dance?"

Kirsty and F looked like the dogs in the fairytale:

Kirsty's eyes were the size of saucers, and F's were the size of dinner plates.

Kirsty began to giggle. "Oh, Anna," she shook her head helplessly, "I *told* you you'd knock 'em dead, and you did. But I never thought you'd knock *Foster Addams* dead. Isn't he the most gorgeous guy you've ever seen?"

"Not bad," I admitted. Of course, to me Foster Addams could never compare with F, but there was no doubt that he was a nice-looking young man.

"*Not bad!*" Kirsty squealed in protest. "*Not bad!* I absolutely thought I'd die when I heard you ask him to dance. I tried to rescue you, but . . ."

"Yes, I saw you," I agreed, rather tartly. "Only pausing for a moment to blink your eyes and drop your jaw on the way to liberate me."

Kirsty blushed. "Well, you were busy dancing with Foster and they *asked*, so —"

I turned to F and repeated my request. "F? You said you would dance with me. Will you?" I held out my hand.

"I — sure, A. Sure I will," he said. He took my hand in his and gingerly placed his other hand on the small of my back.

"Um," he said. "I'm not very good at this, A. Not as good as you, anyway. I was watching you with that Addams guy, and you looked so graceful. And so comfortable, like you'd been doing it all your life." He placed his foot squarely on mine. "Oh, sorry."

"That's quite all right," I said. "Thank you." F didn't seem to know what to do with my hand. "Um," he said, standing there awkwardly and shifting back and forth.

"Just relax, F," I advised him, "and listen to the music. It'll tell you what to do."

"Oh, okay," he said humbly.

I snuggled in a little closer to him. He tightened his grip and began to move slowly to the music.

The events of the evening had made me reckless. I decided to take advantage of the fact that F seemed a bit befogged. I closed my eyes and laid my head on his chest. He was shorter than Foster, so my forehead rested at the base of his throat. I could hear his heartbeat, feel the movement of his ribs as he breathed. It was heaven.

Slowly I felt the tension drain out of him. He moved more naturally and held me with more authority.

"A?" he said after a while, "Did you like him? Foster Addams, I mean."

I considered. "Yes, I did," I said finally. "I think he's a nice person."

This reply seemed to sink him in gloom. Probably he would have preferred to hear that Andrea's beloved was a thoroughly nasty person. Then F could think how much better he would be as a boyfriend for Andrea than Foster.

As if to confirm my guess, he sighed deeply. I tried valiantly to rejoice that F's love was doomed, but to no avail. That sigh cut me like a knife. I searched for something to cheer him up.

"I'm not sure that he likes Andrea that much, to tell you the truth," I said. "He called her 'Cast-Iron Andrea,' which *might* be a compliment, I suppose, but the way he said it, it didn't sound very affectionate."

"I know," he said. "I heard him."

This didn't appear to make things any better. Maybe he was annoyed that anyone would speak scoffingly of Andrea.

"He seemed to like *you* all right," F said at last. He sounded rather hostile. I pulled away from F's chest in order to look up at his face in surprise.

"Oh, but —" I said helplessly, trying to explain what was so obvious to me, "it wasn't *me* he liked. It was the costume."

"So what you're telling me is that if he'd found that dress laid out on a chair somewhere, he'd have picked it up and complimented it and kissed it and danced with it *three* times?"

"No, no," I said, shaking my head impatiently. F wasn't usually this dense. "I mean that I was in disguise; it wasn't me. He doesn't know me, he doesn't know anything about me. He thinks I'm a flirt and a heartbreaker, and how much more wrong can you get than that? If you don't know that I'm shy, you don't know anything about me."

"Then I guess I don't know anything about you," he said, with a meaningful stare.

"What do you mean, F?" I asked, completely bewildered.

"You *did* flirt with him. I saw you. And you liked it, the way he had his hands all over you." F sounded positively savage.

"I *didn't!*" I cried, outraged.

"Did too!" he said childishly, his voice climbing an octave. He seemed close to tears.

Dawn broke abruptly over my mental horizon. "Why, F," I said, before I could stop myself, "you're *jealous.*"

"Me?" F demanded. "Of you? And Foster Addams? Don't flatter yourself."

Crushed, I subsided into silence. My new-found confidence collapsed like a pricked balloon. *Fool! Idiot!* My hand crept up to my mouth, and I bit my finger hard to punish myself for my stupid self-deceiving vanity and pride. Great splashy tears began to roll down my face, smearing my makeup.

F was muttering something, his whole body stiff with repressed emotion. When the song was over, he broke away without apology and marched off in the opposite direction.

"Anna, what's the matter? Why are you crying?" It was Kirsty.

"F! Oh, F!" I sobbed like a little girl.

"What did he do to you? Did Francis upset you? He did, didn't he? I'll kill him." And off Kirsty went to kill F.

"No, no," I moaned weakly. "Don't kill him. Don't kill F, Kirsty." I sank, weeping, into a heavily cobwebbed chair.

If, I thought, I got up and walked very quietly through the house into the kitchen, I could slip into the broom closet. I could reenter my own safe world and never, ever come out again. I'd barricade the entrances so F and Kirsty couldn't get in.

Then I'd — I'd start burrowing underground. I would build myself a city underground, all for myself. That's what I'll do, I thought. If I can just summon up the strength to stand up and walk through these crowds of people out to the kitchen. In just a minute, that's what I'm going to do.

"Excuse me? I'm sorry, but I'm afraid you'll have to leave."

I looked up. A large, solid-looking man stood there before me. Mr. Albright.

Now what?

seventeen

"Leave?" I stared up at him. Was I being thrown out of the house into the street?

Evidently I was.

"I'm sorry," he repeated firmly, not sounding sorry at all. "You've really upset Andrea. I've never seen her like this, she's practically in hysterics. And she tells me that she never invited you to the party. She says she doesn't even know who you are."

"She does *too!*" I burst out.

"Oh?" Mr. Albright's voice was cold. "Well, I suggest that you two pursue your feud some other time. And now —" He reached out to grab my arm so he could escort me forcibly out of the door.

I eluded him, almost vaulting out of the chair, my heart pounding. How I longed for my lost invisibility! Always before I had felt small and insignificant compared to others; now I felt as though I had grown monstrously large, a bloated, fleshy giantess trembling foolishly before him.

"I — I'm Kirsty's friend," I stammered.

"Oh." Mr. Albright seemed somewhat disconcerted, but then he rallied. "What's your name? I'll tell her you've gone home. Do you have a ride?"

"No, no, I haven't," I murmured, my mind racing. *Hidehidehide* screamed every instinct I owned. But once again, I could not hide. I remembered what F had said about his father hunting me down, and I was paralyzed with fear.

Mr. Albright sighed. "I'll take you home. Where do you live?"

I simply gaped at him.

Evidently Mr. Albright had decided that I was simple-minded. "Okay, let's start with the basics. What . . . is . . . your . . . name?" he said loudly, enunciating each word carefully.

"My name?" I asked, stalling for time.

Unfortunately, this seemed to irritate him.

"Now listen here, young lady, I've about had enough of you. Tell me your name and where you live, or I'll simply boot you out of the door. You can't behave like this in other people's houses, you know."

The injustice of this made me gasp aloud. A sudden fury swept over me.

"You — you —" I struggled for utterance, and finally managed, "You should talk! How — how *dare* you!"

Mr. Albright's brow darkened. He hadn't been exactly sunny-looking before, but now he resembled a tornado about to smash a small town to smithereens.

"And what, precisely, do you mean by that?" he demanded.

Mad with rage and grief, I rolled on, disregarding the dangerous edge to his voice.

"What right do you have to order people out of this house? It isn't yours. You don't even live here. You're not — not even related to the Newlands!" my voice caught with a sob. "And if my father knew how you were talking to me he'd — he'd —" I faltered, unable to imagine what my gentle, shy father would have done to avenge this affront to his daughter.

For some reason, Mr. Albright looked less angry after this outburst.

"I'm going to marry Mrs. Newland," he explained in a quieter tone. "That gives me a right."

"You can't," I said stubbornly. "Mr. Newland isn't dead."

Mr. Albright frowned. He looked at me a little oddly.

"Mr. Newland was presumed dead three years ago," he said.

"That doesn't mean that he is!" I protested.

"Do you have any evidence that he isn't?" Mr. Albright had stopped treating me like I was stupid, at least. He asked me seriously, as one adult to another.

"No, but — do you have any evidence that he is?"

"Well, no, not direct evidence. But I do have evidence that he is dead so far as this family is concerned."

"What do you mean?"

"I mean that any father who loved his family, or even had the slightest concern for their feelings, would have gotten in touch over the past eleven years."

"But what if he had amnesia?" I burst out. "What if he got hit on the head and forgot all about his family? That wouldn't mean he didn't love them." This had long seemed like a possible explanation to me.

"Is that what Kirsty thinks?" Mr. Albright asked. He had sat down in a chair facing me and no longer looked quite so intimidating.

"Kirsty?" I said, puzzled as to why we should be discussing Kirsty. "I'm not sure."

"You can tell Kirsty that if her father *did* have amnesia — and I should add that such extensive, long-lasting amnesia is pretty rare — he's made a new life for himself by now. He may have another wife, a whole other family."

I stood silent, horrified by this idea. That possibility had never occurred to me. "But — what if he remembered suddenly? He could leave them and come back to his first family."

"I doubt it." Mr. Albright shook his head. "After eleven years, it would be the needs and rights of the second family that would seem far more important.

Don't forget that the first family has been getting along without him for over a decade."

I began to cry again, noiselessly, the tears slowly rolling down over my face and my neck and into the bodice of my dress.

"Have you lost your father too?" Mr. Albright inquired gently.

"I — yes. Yes, I have."

"It's a very painful thing to happen," he said.

I nodded.

Hesitantly he reached out a hand and patted mine.

"Some injuries take a long time to heal," he said somberly. "They seem to be fine on the surface, but there's always a tender place under the skin. Listen — what was your name?"

"Anna," I said absently, wiping my tears away with the back of my hand.

"Listen, Anna. If you care about Kirsty, and it sounds like you do, I hope you'll be glad for her. About this marriage, I mean. I think I can be a good father to her and Andrea, and a good husband to their mother."

I was silent for a long time, thinking. Finally I said, "So you think he's dead? Really and truly?"

"It's hard for me to believe that the father of Kirsty and Andrea and the husband of Mrs. Newland would just go away and never write or call or come for eleven years. So, yes, I think he's dead."

I sighed. "Yes. Yes, I suppose you're right."

He smiled. "Now, shall I take you home, or do you want to stay a little while longer? Here comes Kirsty."

I looked up. There was Kirsty, face white as salt, her eyes shifting from me to Mr. Albright.

"Oh, please, let me stay," I begged. "I won't go near Andrea, I swear it."

"Sure, stay a while. But you're right, it might be better to keep away from Andrea. If you've been suggesting that her father is about to stage a return from the dead, that might explain why she's so shook up. Kirsty, your friend Anna here has been giving Andrea a bit of a fright. Why don't you take her up to your room?"

Kirsty nodded vigorously and grabbed me by the wrist.

"Come *on*, Anna," she said and dragged me out of the chair and away from Mr. Albright.

"Wait!" I stopped and dug in my heels. I looked back at Mr. Albright speculatively.

"Yes?" he said, seeing me looking at him.

I stared at him for a long moment, measuring him with my eyes.

"Um . . . do you like your dress slacks with or without cuffs?" I asked.

"Excuse me?" He sounded rather startled.

"Your dress slacks. Some men seem to like them with cuffs and some without. And how about your shirts?" I asked, my imagination beginning to take fire, "Do you prefer button-down or plain? You look," I said, now happily launched on a whole new winter wardrobe, "like someone who wears a three-piece suit to work."

"*Anna! Come on right now!*"

And Kirsty dragged me away. It seemed as though I had spent the whole evening being dragged around by the wrist.

"Kirsty," I asked as we began to mount the stairs, "is he dead?"

"Is who dead?" Kirsty halted halfway up and stared at me.

My mind was in such a turmoil, I wasn't entirely sure which "he" I had been inquiring about, whether I meant F or our father.

"F," I decided. After all, I reasoned, if our father was dead he had probably died a long time ago, while F might still be lying in a pool of blood somewhere on the premises. "You didn't — hurt him, did you, Kirsty?"

"I'd *like* to hurt him," she said ominously. "No, I couldn't find him. Maybe he walked home."

I sighed, half with relief that he was safe from Kirsty's vengeance, and half with sorrow for the unhappy love, which had undoubtedly sent him home alone.

"And to think," Kirsty went on, "that I was actually almost pleased at getting him for a stepbrother. He seemed semihuman."

"Please, Kirsty," I begged, *"please* don't hurt F."

Kirsty looked at me in silence for a moment.

"One of the reasons I liked him," she said, "was that *you* seemed to like him."

I looked down at my feet and said nothing.

Evidently she read something in my face because she exploded. "That stinking rat! And he made you cry. He *knows* how rough this is on you."

"Well," I said, struggling to be fair, "it isn't very hard to make me cry."

"There he is, talking to Andrea. Don't worry," she reassured me, starting back down the stairs, "I won't lay a finger on him."

"But, Kirsty —" I objected, following along in her wake.

"What do you mean, 'That's Anna'?" demanded a voice below us. "What would *you* know about Anna?"

It was Andrea's voice, threatening to soar into hysterics at any moment. "Mother!" Andrea cried, looking wildly about herself, "This kid here says that girl is Anna. There! That girl right there on the stairs!" She pointed accusingly, and once again a whole roomful of people turned to stare at me as I stood, elevated for their inspection on the staircase. "It's not! It can't be!"

Andrea looked terrible, her hair mussed up and her face swollen and red with tears. Mother, Mr. Albright, and F stood behind her. Mother had one hand on

Andrea's shoulder, apparently trying to calm her, but like everyone else, she was looking up at me.

Mother! I thought, and my hand made a little involuntary gesture toward her. But I couldn't, no, I just couldn't. I wrenched my arm away from Kirsty and ran away, up the stairs.

They ran after me.

eighteen

Like a pack of hounds in full cry after a rabbit, they came. I heard the sound of my name being called, of many feet pounding up the stairs behind me.

"Hey!"

"Hey, Anna!"

Thud, thud, thud.

"Darling, come back!" That was Mother, I thought.

"Anna!" Kirsty, sounding impatient.

"Stop her! Make her come back here!" That was Andrea, her voice imperious, sounding out loud and clear above the others.

Thud, thud, thud.

"Who *is* this Anna?" Mr. Albright, sounding mystified.

"Catch her!" An unknown voice.

"Who?"

"The girl in the green dress!"

"Why?"

"I dunno, Andrea wants her."

"She's getting away!"

The thudding swelled to thunder, as the old staircase swayed and groaned under many running feet, like a ship in a gale.

"Oh, A," I heard F's voice, small and far away in the tumult, "I'm so sorry."

The attic door. If I could make it to the attic door before they burst in upon me, I would be perfectly safe. I could slam the door in their faces and lock them away forever. And it was so close! Only twenty feet or so from the head of the stairs.

I rounded the turn and then achieved the top. The door was just there, to the right.

Directly in front of it stood a boy and a girl, arms wrapped tightly about each other, heads lifted like startled deer.

"Out of my way," I ordered brusquely.

They merely gazed at me with wide, astonished eyes.

"There she is!" The leaders of the pack had breasted the top of the stairs and were baying almost at my heels.

I turned and ran in the opposite direction. Back through the upstairs hall, into the old nursery, and hence into the servants' quarters. There was a back stairway, down to the kitchen. I could slip back into my world through the broom closet in the kitchen. I flung myself down the narrow stairs, careless of falling,

175

careless of the racket I was making, careless of everything but reaching sanctuary.

The kitchen was full of people. Evidently not everyone had participated in the chase. A whole group of people were standing around drinking sodas and eating corn chips. Someone had spilled most of the bag of chips on the floor. The broom closet door was open, and a boy was rooting around in it looking for a broom and dustpan with which to clean up the mess.

How could I possibly walk into the broom closet and close the door in front of all these people? The couple upstairs had been bad enough. There were at least ten people here, staring at me, at my wild eyes and frantic face. And the door to the broom closet didn't lock.

Gasping and pressing a hand to my aching side, I fled once again. Past the breakfast room, the laundry room, the scullery, through the butler's pantry, into the dining room, and so to the hall once more. The doorways to the billiard room, the back parlor, the front parlor, the library, all flashed by me. There were people all over, staring at me, pointing at me. And always behind, I heard the shouts of my pursuers, coming ever closer.

They were in the hall now, right behind me. There was nowhere to go. There was literally nowhere to go.

"Oh, help me! Help me," I sobbed, and turned the knob on the front door. It opened slowly, ponderously, as if it were a slab of stone rather than oak. When at last it stood open, I plunged through it, out onto the porch and down the front steps.

After seven years I was once again outside of the house.

It was dark; a flame-lit, dancing darkness. Kirsty had been at work in our front yard as well. Little pumpkins, twenty or thirty of them, were dotted about everywhere, yellow candlelight flickering through wicked, grinning little faces. The street light outside our house was on, and the porch light as well. A swollen, golden moon hung high above me.

I stopped; I stood still, breathing painfully. Where was I to go? I shivered violently. Dressed as I was, I would probably be found dead of exposure tomorrow morning. Ironic, really. Tomorrow, November first, was the Day of the Dead. Dead on the Day of the Dead, I thought idiotically. I turned around to bid a last farewell to my beloved house. It could not protect me now.

And they all came pouring out of the door.

I didn't run. I couldn't. While I kept in pretty good shape crawling through heating ducts and so on, I didn't have the lungs for this sort of activity. Also, my dress was too tight for easy movement.

They stopped too and stood panting and staring at me. It was a smaller group than I had thought: Mother, Kirsty, Andrea, and three strange boys, and in the back, F.

"It's — it's you, Anna," Mother said wonderingly.

At that moment, Mr. Albright appeared. He pushed his way through the little crowd on the front steps.

"Exactly what do you people think you're doing to this poor girl?" he demanded, in a low, intense voice. He stood in front of me, shielding me from their eyes.

"Elaine?" He turned to my mother. "What the hell is this all about, anyway? Why is everybody chasing this girl through the house like a gang of wild hyenas? If she's done something wrong, let's discuss it in a civilized manner instead of scaring her half to death. Elaine?"

"It's Anna," my mother said. "After all these years, it's Anna. And — and she's all grown up!" Mother burst into noisy tears.

"Look, Mom," Kirsty said eagerly. "You can *see* her now."

"Yes," Mother wept, "I see."

Mr. Albright was clearly bewildered, and he was not a man to enjoy being in that condition.

"Will somebody please tell me," he growled, swinging on me with a menacing expression, "*Who is this girl?*"

Kirsty and Mother both spoke at once.

"She's —" Kirsty began.

"Frank, that's my —" Mother said. They both stopped in confusion.

Mother, I saw, was willing to claim me.

"Andrea could tell you," I suggested diffidently.

Andrea stared at me for a moment, expressionless. At last she spoke.

"That's Anna," she admitted.

"Oh, Frank, it's *Anna!*" Mother sobbed.

"I *know* that," Mr. Albright snapped irritably. "But who *is* Anna?"

"Anna is my sister," Andrea said.

Mr. Albright looked blank, as though he wasn't following the conversation.

"Hey, cool!" said one of the three strange boys.

"My *little* sister," Andrea continued, "though that may not be so obvious." She turned to Mother. "Do you think she should be allowed to dress like that when she's only fourteen years old?"

"I think she looks lovely," Mother said, smiling through her tears.

"Me too," offered another of the three strange boys.

"That's not exactly the point, Ma," said Andrea sulkily.

Mr. Albright closed his mouth, which had been hanging open. He cleared his throat.

"Perhaps we should go back inside the house and discuss this. It sounds like you've got some explaining to do, Elaine."

"Yes," my mother said, smiling radiantly. "I do. Lots of explaining. I'm so sorry, Frank," she said, turning a beaming face on him. "I *couldn't* tell you before. I wanted to, but you would have thought I was crazy. I mean, *I* thought I was crazy. But I'm not. I'm not crazy. Oh, Anna, please, please let me give you a hug."

Shyly I submitted. It was strange, being embraced by my mother, but after spending what seemed like hours in the arms of one man after another, it was less of a novelty than it might have been earlier. I even hugged her back a little bit.

We went back into the house. I looked back over my shoulder at the autumn night I had visited so briefly. It was rather beautiful, I thought; unlike the terrifying daylit world, it did not give a sense of infinite space. It seemed a secret, private place, with deep shadows between the pools of lamp light. It was a place where I could go, a place I could walk in unafraid, until I grew accustomed to the wide world.

Mr. Albright scolded the three boys, who were showing a good deal of interest in this new development in our family, and sent them home. Then he sent everybody else at the party home.

Once the hubbub of leave-taking was over, once Mr. Albright had scoured through the house three times, flushing out an impromptu saxophone recital in the front parlor, as well as assorted couples kissing in the laundry room, the linen closet, and the breakfast room, Mother explained.

She explained all about me right up until the moment I disappeared into the wall. Her recitation was interrupted periodically by a series of mini-explosions of disbelief and consternation from Mr. Albright, but she persevered to the end. When Mother finished, F, blushing hotly, explained about our correspondence.

"But, Francis," Mr. Albright protested, looking as though events had gotten a bit beyond his control, "how did you even know she existed?"

"I didn't." He looked miserably at me. I rescued him.

"He didn't. He just wrote a note and stuck it in the wall for the fun of it, thinking maybe someday somebody would find it."

"Yeah," F agreed, nodding enthusiastically. "Like putting a note in a bottle and throwing it in the ocean. Kind of a neat idea, I always thought."

Andrea rolled her eyes.

"F — that is, Francis — has a very romantic nature," I defended him.

"Pff!" Andrea made a contemptuous noise with her lips.

"And you're telling me you've been living in some kind of a little hole in the walls all this time," said Mr. Albright incredulously.

"*Not* a little hole," I contradicted him.

"Oh, Anna, it was too a little hole." Kirsty shook her head at me.

"But — you never saw the rest of it. You don't know —" I stopped. They would never see, never know the full extent of my achievement. They were too big to travel through my passages. Even I was too big. I sighed.

"It wasn't little," I said sadly. "It was the whole world to me."

I was banished from that world forever, I knew. I couldn't go back now. One day soon I would go away from here entirely; I would leave this house, perhaps never to return.

I hugged myself, comforting my fear. Very well then, I thought, I will be my own house. I will build myself a house out of my own flesh and bones where my frightened child-self can find shelter. After all, isn't that one of the things that women do? We are houses for our children, until they are strong enough to breathe and walk alone. Someday I may carry a baby inside me, shielding it from harm within the stronghold of my body. So surely I must be able to give myself shelter now.

"At least F will be with me. He'll give me courage," I thought, and then blushed as I realized that I had spoken aloud.

"No, he won't," said Kirsty.

"Only in the summer," F said. "I'm supposed to live with my mother during the school year."

This was a blow! I dropped my eyes and bit my lip, trying to control the tears that threatened to spill over. Surely I was old enough by now to stop crying all the time.

"Um, we could," F mumbled, not meeting my eyes, "we could write. Letters, you know. Or e-mail. My Dad gave me a computer this year for my birthday. And he has one, so there'd be one in Chicago for you to use. I bet you'd be really good at computers."

"Yes," I agreed, "we could write. I don't know anything about computers, of course, but I'd be happy to learn."

In a way, that was better. We would write letters and tell each other things. This time I could be me, Anna, and not someone else. I could probably send him packages through the mail, too. And then there would be the whole summer together.

It *was* better. To tell you the truth, I don't think I'm ready for the things Kirsty claims that men and women do together. We could be friends for now, until I learned more about this business of being a woman. And then, some day . . .

"You could write to Andrea, too," I said generously.

F made a funny movement with his shoulders, sort of a combination of a shrug and a shudder.

"I don't think I will," he said, "I'd rather write to you. Anna —" he hesitated and then went on. "I'm sorry I told Andrea who you were. I was just sucking up to her, hoping she'd notice me. I didn't know they'd chase you like that. I guess that must have been pretty scary for you." I nodded fervently, and he said discontentedly, "And then she called me 'this kid' like she didn't even know who I was. I guess it was a shock and all, but still. I don't think I like Andrea as much as I did."

"Oh, Andrea's not bad," I said charitably. "When you get to know her."

"Well, anyway, I'm sorry for being such a creep tonight."

"That's okay," I said.

Mr. Albright, who had been conferring in a huddle with Mother for the past few minutes, approached me cautiously, eyeing me as though I might bite if not handled properly.

"Your mother tells me that you've never attended school," he said. "Can you, uh, read?"

Kirsty snorted.

I nodded.

"Well, that's great!" he said heartily. "Wonderful. But you see, Anna, just knowing how to read isn't enough. You're going to have to get some schooling in. Now, I thought that in the light of your, um, previous history, you might prefer to be tutored at home. We could probably manage a private tutor, if you'd like."

I considered. Mother watched me nervously, remembering the last time we discussed the subject of my education.

"Yes," I said at last. "I think I would like a private tutor at first. But eventually I'd like to go to school like other girls." I snuck a peek at F to see if he was suitably impressed with my courage. He was.

"If you feel up to it, I suppose that would be all right," said Mr. Albright, sounding worried. "Chicago's a big city. We'll have to find the right school, the right neighborhood."

"Don't worry, Dad," said F. "If Anna says she'll do something, she will."

I smiled complacently.

"Anna," Mother said, "You look tired. It's getting late. And you too, Kirsty, aren't you tired?"

"No, not at all," she said, through a huge yawn.

"Come on, girls, to bed," Mother said. "Oh! I wonder — I hope there are sheets on Anna's old bed. Let's go have a look. Kirsty! Bed time."

"Oh, okay," Kirsty said crossly. "Let's go, Anna."

At the door I stopped and looked back at Mr. Albright.

"Uh, yes?" he inquired.

"About those dress shirts —" I began, but Kirsty grabbed me by the wrist again and pulled.

"Come *on*, Anna!"

And that really *is* all there is to tell. So far, anyway.